# Mona

Eva R. Bird

For information contact :
Eva R. Bird
monathebook@gmail.com

ISBN: 978-0-9666679-9-8

# Acknowledgments

**FIRST OF ALL,** I want to thank my editor, Lea Agnew, whose wisdom and patience assisted me as we ventured into an exciting experience which was relatively unexplored by either of us.

My three adult children have been my cheering squad along this tedious journey: Anika, my prayer partner; her spouse, Alan D. Jones, (himself the author of four books); my son, Shaka, who believes that I have boundless imagination; and Lesley, my relentless administrative assistant, who refused to allow me to slack up.

I am grateful to Nicole Austin and Philura Williams, who worked on the edit, and Anja Williams, whose creative skills are manifested in the book cover and layout. Thank you to Dee Turner, Nia Brown, Alicia Thomas, and my two Judys (Warren and Harper) who have blessed me with their encouragement and prayers.

Most of all, I thank our great and merciful God for bringing me thus far in faith.

# Table of Contents

EVA R. BIRD

To my two oldest sisters, Doris and Mabel, who have always encouraged me to put my thoughts on paper.

# *Prologue*

## RETURN TO REANEY STREET

**AS MONA APPROACHED THE CORNER** on the arm of her son Adam, she could see that the street sign still stood where 10th Street joined Reaney Street. Remarkably, it had survived nearly a century of relentless buffeting by rainstorms, snowstorms and hurricanes. The sight of that sign allayed her concern that she might be at the wrong mound of grass. Mona knew she had indeed returned to the place where she first learned to walk, run and cry.

Yet so much was gone. There was no trace of the country store that had helped the family survive the throes of poverty. And where, she wondered, were the three silver-leaf maple trees that adorned the front yard? Or the mulberry tree which had ripped her dress while she climbed, resulting in punishment that she still remembered painfully.

Mona was actually glad to see that the weeping willow was gone. It had stood near her bedroom window, providing a path for caterpillars to crawl in and leave painful whelps over her body. All told, there was only one familiar object in sight – a rusty old iron wash tub in what had been her Aunt Lillie's yard. Now filled with leaves and decayed animal refuse, it was an odd souvenir of a bygone time.

Where was the fence, she wondered? What had become of the steel fence and gates that had kept Mona, her sisters and brother securely imprisoned for decades?

Adam realized that his mother's knees were paining her when he saw her shift her position on her cane, the one he and his sisters had finally persuaded her to use after several falls. But to that day she hadn't quite learned how to use it as a buttress for her left knee.

"Mama, maybe we should leave now. You probably need to rest before dinner," Adam said.

Mona sighed. "My son, where did the years go? All of my family has passed and yet as I stand here they are all so tangibly present with me. I know we were not the closest family ever, but I believe that they are holding my seat in Heaven."

Adam responded with a warm embrace. He adored his mother. At age 61 he still loved to hear her tell the story of his birth, how she had given praises to God as he lay on her breasts.

Mona continued, "Yet I know that life has moved on and that God has blessed me with a long life and many descendants. For His loving kindness and tender mercies I give Him praise."

Walking slowly back toward the car, she turned once again for a last glance at the street sign. The markings of time made strange patterns on its face. Mona could swear she saw what looked like a smile. Glancing up at the interstate bridge, she realized that all physical evidence of her early life would have been obliterated, had it not been for that adamant street sign that refused to be destroyed.

# Chapter One

## NOTHING BUT CHARACTER

**NOT UNTIL MONA WAS** 47 years old had she dared to challenge the myth surrounding the Randall family legacy. Her family had worked so hard and successfully to portray an image of love and unity to the watching world. Somehow they had grown to believe this image themselves. No "illegitimate" babies, no incarcerations, no police records. It was believed up and down Reaney Street and throughout the neighborhood that the Randalls had "nothing but character."

But in conversation with her two oldest sisters not long after their mother's passing, Mona shocked them by frankly admitting her feelings. "I cannot really accept the notion that we were a close-knit family".

Stella, eight years her senior, showed instant irritation. "Mona, please don't talk like that. Momma and Poppa would be very disturbed if they could hear you."

Mona hastily replied. "I loved my parents. I hold no ill feelings toward them. At the same time I cannot remember growing up in a happy environment. I felt instant approval if I said or did anything pleasing to my parents and siblings, but if I committed displeasing acts, rejection was evident like a loss of love."

Stella was obviously shaken by her younger sister's words. "We need to forget it. It's all in the past now. Let bygones be bygones".

Mona wondered if Stella was struggling with a sense of guilt in her failure to tell her mother goodbye. Only Mona and her sister Erica had been there at the end.

Laura, the second oldest of the siblings, was evidently not ready to forget unpleasant childhood memories. "Poppa was so cruel to us. He seemed to have had no energy to love and cherish us. He wasn't even able to love his wife." She winced as if, while speaking, she was feeling the pain from her father's switches that had curled around her body.

Mona believed she understood each of her sisters' strong reactions. Stella had buried the pain deeply so she would not have to face it, while Laura didn't seem able to forgive her parents even after so many years. This realization convinced Mona to cut off further discussion. She excused herself to retrieve her mail from the post office and then hurried home. She had stirred up emotions in herself, too, forcing recollections of a past that might well have remained buried forever beneath unexplored feelings. Maybe that would have been best, she thought to herself.

A few hours later, Mona and her daughter Priscilla were left together at the dinner table. "Mommy why are you so quiet tonight?" Priscilla asked. Priscilla's eyes never left her mother's face, deep in reflection.

"My thoughts have been racing since I left your Aunt Stella and Aunt Laura today."

Priscilla instantly stood upright in a combative stance.

"Why, Momma? Did they say something to upset you?"

"No, no my dear. Please, can we drop the subject?"

Priscilla was the youngest of Mona's three children. She fussed over her mother constantly, a habit acquired while watching her mother fight a near fatal illness several years before. The illness had been a monumental turning point in Mona's life, but for her daughter, it had been a frightful brush with her mother's mortality. Priscilla dropped the conversation but remained watchful.

Mona could sense her concern. She excused herself from the dinner table and went directly to her bedroom. After spending an hour in prayer, she tossed and turned as bittersweet memories swirled in her mind. They took her back to the past, back to half-forgotten events, back to reality, back to reevaluating that long-cherished family legacy of "nothing but character."

\* \* \*

# Chapter Two
## FAMILY MIGRATION

**THE RANDALL FAMILY HAD** rural southern roots, but by Mona's adulthood they had lived in the Northeast for decades and adopted its urban ways. Like tens of thousands of African American families, they had taken part in an historic exodus in the 1920s that promised better economic prospects and escape from the legally sanctioned segregation and oppression of the Jim Crow South. As was true of many of these migrants, Mona's parents had two strong advantages: relentless survival instincts and no fear of hard work.

Although Mona's early memories were of Chester, Pennsylvania, she had drawn her first breath in rural South Georgia in a 4-bedroom farmhouse near a village called Dixie. Mona was the youngest of Madeline and Josiah Randall's six children, and the family moved north when she was six months old. They were drawn by favorable reports from relatives who already had settled in Chester and seemed to be prospering.

Although Mona never thought of Dixie as home, the community of her birth would always be vivid in her mind. Her family returned often to visit the numerous relatives still living there. Growing up, Mona always looked forward to the trips both for the adventures of travel and because Madeline's mother doted on her. One trip in particular made an impression because her father Josiah had accompanied them, which was a rarity.

"How y'all making out up north?" Daddy Randall had asked Josiah with his characteristic bellow. Years of chewing tobacco had stained the few teeth Daddy Randall had left.

"Everything is good, Papa," Josiah replied. He knew better than to admit to his father that he often second guessed his judgment about taking his family north. He would never want Daddy Randall to know how hard it was to provide enough food to feed his family.

"Yo wife is sickly," Daddy Randall observed.

"She don't feel too well most days," Josiah acknowledged. "But she goes to work five days a week." Josiah knew his father would understand what he meant – the line between sickly and true illness was whether you could drag yourself to work.

Mama Randall said little and took no notice of Madeline's poor health. But Madeline's own mother noted her decline and addressed it directly. "Maddy you need to come back down here so I can take care of you," she insisted.

Madeline tried to reassure her. "I'll be all right. Josiah is trying so hard to make ends meet."

Mona would long remember something else about that trip. With both her parents "back home" in a familiar atmosphere, the normally ragged edges of their relationship seemed to smooth out a bit – especially when they went fishing at a local lake where they used to court. Something about the quietness and stillness of the setting seemed to restore the original and gentle bond between them, which their children rarely saw.

The Randall children adored their mother but resented their father for being callous and unloving to them and Madeline. No matter how much his wife attended to his every wish, he refused to be pleased. She even spoon-fed him at the kitchen table.

"Poppa do you love me?" she would ask plaintively.
"Not a bit,"
"You do love me!"
"I said it and I mean it, nary a bit!"

Madeline loved Josiah deeply and even though she had heard his harsh words before, they broke her heart with each repeating. In the beginning the relationship between them had been quite different.

They had met when Madeline was 17. She was the 7th child in the Braxton family, which would eventually total 15.

Growing up had been hard. When not in school, the Braxton children either toiled on the family farm or did chores around the house. Sunday was the only day of rest, but it came with restrictions on playing outdoors, reading comic books or enjoying card games. After church services (which might last an entire day), the children were told to check their homework and prepare for school the next day. Even chores like washing and ironing were forbidden on "the Lord's day."

Madeline loved school and welcomed its challenges. She developed a lifelong passion for reading and poured over any book or magazine that came into her hands. Naturally bright, she graduated from the 8th grade and began teaching in that same three-room schoolhouse she had attended since 1st grade.

She met Josiah at a church revival. He was sweet and shy when he approached her and held out his hand.

"Hello. My name is Josiah Randall. Ain't you one of the Braxton girls that lives in the big farmhouse down the road?"

"Yes, my name is Madeline."

"I see you when I drive past your house, once or twice a month, to get groceries from Brookline Country Store. I hate that ride cause it takes darn near four hours to get there and back...my donkey's so old and that road's tore up. And Lord don't let it rain! Seeing you is the only thing I look forward to."

Madeline looked sympathetic and bashful. "You know the little lake about a quarter mile from my house? My family fishes there. You could stop there to rest and water your donkey sometime."

Josiah smiled. "Thanks for letting me know. I'll look for it on my next trip."

From that point on, Josiah could frequently be seen riding past her farmhouse driving his donkey-drawn wagon. As she suggested, he would stop by the lake to rest. Each time, he would leave a small gift for Madeline, which she was able to retrieve without her parents noticing.

A romance blossomed between them, and six weeks later Josiah knocked on Madeline's door with raindrops dripping from his threadbare jacket. Madeline introduced him to her parents. They were also impressed by his shy and winsome charm.

Six months later Madeline became his bride. Josiah took her to live with him and his parents, Harry and Isabel Randall.

From the very first day Madeline could tell that her mother-in-law was going to be difficult. The woman never smiled.

The Randall's large farmhouse was home to ten siblings, five of whom had brought their spouses and children back into the family home. "Daddy Harry" was cruel, and his grandchildren lived in constant fear whenever in his presence. Even Josiah accepted his father's authority without protest or question.

After months of living in the dour home, Madeline escaped through a frightening experience that she looked back on later as divine providence. One day, while sitting on a stump in the yard shelling black eyed peas, she turned her body slightly to relieve the ache in her back. This small move saved her from the axe held by Josiah's brother, Jake, aimed straight for her head. Her screaming brought family members running. Jake, the family agreed, acted "queer" at times and should be avoided. Within the family the acceptance of his bizarre behavior troubled Madeline. She forced the issue with her husband.

"Josiah, we have to leave here right now!"

"We can't leave right now, Maddy." I need more time to work on Mr. Faucett's field so we can build a house".

"I want to leave here right now!" Madeline cried. "I'm pregnant with your child and I don't want to live in fear of losing my life or our baby's".

Josiah was stunned. As he gave her a lukewarm embrace, he thought it strange that he should first learn about his unborn child at a time like this, instigated by Jake's aberrant behavior.

He knew that Madeline would indeed leave him if he attempted to keep her in his parent's home. Should she depart without him, Josiah would lose the respect of his parents. He also knew he couldn't abide living with her family. So Josiah and Madeline found work as sharecroppers and lived on their own. It was a hard life, but Madeline much preferred it to the threat of sudden death from her demented brother-in-law.

Over the next eight years Madeline bore Josiah five daughters and a son. Each time she went directly from the field to the bed to give birth – except one that wouldn't wait for her to make it inside. In that case, she miscarried soon after realizing she was pregnant, but she was far enough along to know it was a male. He would have been her fourth child.

Working as a sharecropper to feed his growing family exhausted Josiah. His children were too young to work alongside him to ease the burden, and Maddy was showing signs of ill health. Josiah could not help but notice her deep belching.

When their relatives in Chester encouraged them to

come north, he and Madeline packed up the children –
five youngsters and a babe in arms – and moved.

The age span between oldest and youngest was eight
years. The oldest was Stella, and soon behind her came
Laura. They had quite different temperaments, yet they
were inseparable as children. Tempestuous Stella was
quick to anger, but once the storm had passed, she was
skillful at acting as if nothing had happened.

Laura was unusually pretty, and keenly aware of the fact.
She had charm that drew others to follow her lead.

Next came Dimetra, whose ruddy complexion and reddish
hair hinted at what would be a lifelong combative streak.
Placing the newborn in her mother's arms, the nurse
said, "Looks like you have a firebrand on your hands Mrs.
Randall," words which proved true. Dimetra would battle
her way through life. Even as a child, she knew how
to force life to bend to her way. Invoking the legend of
the Pied Piper of Hamelin and his magic pipe, she would
gather up and march dozens of neighborhood children to
Sunday school each week.

Two years behind her was day-dreaming Erica, who lived
vicariously through her books and her imagination. She
was fascinated by the idyllic characters in romance novels

and grew up intent on making their glamorous, carefree lifestyle her own.

Harold was the fifth child and only son. As a baby he had a quiet and peaceful temperament until hunger struck. Madeline was unable to breastfeed him beyond the first few weeks and resorted to feeding him with canned milk and boiled water. By the time it could be prepared, baby Harold would be in a rage. Growing up, he realized that through mercurial changes of mood, he could exercise nearly complete control over his sisters.

Finally came Mona, the one Randall child with no memories of sharecropping hardships as the family's way of life. As is often true of the youngest in a large family, she grew up with a mixed sense of privilege and persecution. She suspected she was her mother's favorite, although Madeline's strict rules were enforced as sternly for Mona as for the older children.

From her siblings, Mona came to understand that she had not been a pretty baby. The older girls noted that Randalls usually were born with a head full of curly hair and wondered why Mona's was "wooly and nappy." The siblings jokingly called her a "little yellow eyed conjurer" because of her small stature and the light tint of her eyes. In spite of such teasing, Mona showed innate confidence and determination from an early age. The Randalls sometimes used an old southern saying, "root little piggy or die," which translated means "you'd best fend for yourself." Madeline and Josiah's youngest child took the saying to heart and grew up with strong survival instincts.

When the Randalls arrived in Chester, the family stayed with relatives for a time. In the custom of that day, the kinfolk pooled resources and talents to help each other build their homes. No one had formal construction training.

The Randall's new wooden frame house had 3 bedrooms, living room, dining room, and kitchen as well as front and back porches. A bathroom was added behind the kitchen many years later, freeing the family from trudging to the outhouse, a particular inconvenience at night.

From the day they moved into the house, frigid air currents and rain found easy entrance. The roof leaked at multiple points, and the family quickly assembled a collection of buckets and tubs to catch the rain as it syncopated on the roof. The house was easily penetrated by bone chilling winds and snow that were a natural part of Chester's northerly climate. When winter weather was intense, an insufficiency of blankets forced the family to sleep in their clothing. It was typical for several family members to suffer with colds at the same time.

During a visit from South Georgia, Madeline's brother Miles installed a fireplace. His main occupation was principal of the community high school, with construction as a side line. Perhaps because harsh winters were rare in South Georgia, building fireplaces did not seem to be his forte. To feel warmth, it was necessary to stand so close as to risk being hit by a spark. The Randall children kept their distance and considered the fireplace more of a danger than a help.

They had been in Chester six years when the Great Depression descended on the country, precipitating the longest economic downturn in America's history. The family was among millions of Americans who found themselves poverty-stricken and desperate for work. After losing his job at the local steel plant, Josiah was obliged to sell roasted peanuts for 5 cents a bag. In spite of poor health, Madeline cleaned houses for $2 a day.

Madeline prayed. Josiah prayed. Mona and her siblings acted out some semblance of prayer. So why, she wondered many years later, had there been so much contention among us?

Although Josiah had never learned to read, he had no problem memorizing certain passages from the Bible. His favorite was the warning in Proverbs - "spare the rod and spoil the child," and he lived up to its admonition. The children's whippings from their father were long and brutal. Mona remembered that she couldn't don enough clothing to buffer the lashes and lessen the pain. "Shut up! Stop that crying! The more you cry the longer I'm gonna whip you!" Even when so warned, the lashings were so harsh and relentless that the Randall children could not suppress their screams.

Although she knew his anger well enough, Mona could not remember ever seeing her father cry. She suspected that at some phase of his childhood he had been told that boys should never resort to tears, regardless of their pain.

In spite of what seemed to her like constant turmoil, the family gathered for prayer meetings every Wednesday night. In addition, every night the children were required to say prayers and repeat a verse from the Bible before retiring.

The fact that there was never quite enough money produced a somber household with frequent quarrels. Josiah seemed to take special pleasure in dampening moments of enjoyment in his children's lives. If he caught them in a card game such as "flinch 'em" or playing scrabble, he would interrupt in some way. Maybe he was irritated by his inability to read and thus to join in. Or maybe he didn't like laughter. Just as she didn't recall him crying, Mona could not remember ever having seen him laugh.

"Stella, get me a cup of tea," he would order his oldest daughter. This was not a simple task. It meant building a fire in the wood stove (provided the wood was dry) to heat the water. Josiah's command for a cup of tea effectively ended any games for the night.

To avoid having their father disrupt their entertainment, the children resorted to running off and hiding the moment they heard his key in the front door. This attempt at escape did not always work because he had an uncanny way of figuring out their retreat location. Josiah's mood at the time determined whether they were in for another lashing.

Madeline had her own trials, the primary one being the prediction of kinfolk in the neighborhood that her five daughters, left alone every day, would turn the place into a nursery. She solicited the aid of those same gossips to keep an eye on the brood.

Mona heard her sisters' complaints about living under the watchful eyes of snooping relatives who seemed to surround them on every side. "I hate it when Cousin Annie Mae hollers at us from her upstairs bedroom window," Stella grumbled. "What about Cousin Lillie? She treats us like dirt," Laura retorted. Mona would never forget when Cousin Lillie had marched over to punish Laura for talking back to her. Lillie entered the yard with a belt in her hand. Laura remained still, with anger surging through her body. She was thinking, "Poppa beats me enough! I won't take it from you." Laura grabbed Cousin Lillie's legs and threw her to the ground, sending her to the hospital! Fortunately the injuries were minor, and Cousin Lillie never came through the Randall gate again.

Madeline's list of "don'ts" for her daughters seemed endless.

"Don't ever go outside the gate for any reason."

"Don't go anywhere alone". (The girls were always together up until the time each was married, with the older daughters chaperoning the younger ones.)

"Don't smoke cigarettes."

"Don't drink wine."

"Don't dance." (That was the work of the devil)

"Don't let a man kiss or embrace you. Your virginity is your most precious possession. If you lose that, you have nothing." When her daughters entertained male friends at home, Madeline would pass through the living room every half hour, believing this would calm any rising passion.

"Don't ever ride in a car with a man alone."

In spite of all the "don'ts" Mona also remembered fun times with her family. Although Madeline had suffered several heart attacks, she still found time to take everyone to the carnival when it came to town. The children were treated to a bag of cotton candy and a ride on the merry-go-round. And every summer the family went on vacation via ferry boat to Waterview Beach.

With, of course, another "don't".

"Don't get too close to the railings! If you fall in that water, the devil will catch you before your eyes close!" As a result of this last admonition, Mona was the only Randall child who ever learned to swim.

For Madeline, keeping her children clear of the devil went

far beyond vacations and boat rides. On Reaney Street, it was an every-day priority – evidenced by the stern metal fence that surrounded the house.

# Chapter Three

## A FENCE TO KEEP THE WORLD OUT

*EVEN AS A SMALL CHILD*, Mona intuitively understood what the fence was about – separating the Randall children from dangers and enticements that Madeline and Josiah felt were lurking outside. Madeline especially was proactive about drawing boundaries around her daughters. Until Stella was of an age to work, the only "outside the fence" activities allowed were school and church.

Looking back in adulthood, Mona realized how much her mother's world had been shadowed by the judgmental attitude of neighbors – and fears that their judgments might prove true. Relatives and friends alike seemed to assume that as the Randall daughters grew up, one by one they would fall prey to worldly temptations, bringing hardship as well as embarrassment to their parents. "As the first one goes, they all go," was the expectation of that time and place.

Madeline was determined that this would not happen in her family, if she could possibly prevent it. Thus, the list of "don'ts" was frequently repeated to her daughters. Moreover, the list was physically and psychologically reinforced by the imposing fence around the house. Mona came to understand the fence as her mother's symbolic line of defense to safeguard the family's reputation (especially the daughters) from "I told you so" verdicts among family and friends.

Following the model of her parents, Stella didn't shy from hard work. When the Depression hit, her family's financial distress forced her to leave school after the 7th grade to take a job. At 17, she was employed as a live-in housekeeper for the Prichard family. It was a bleak existence, and she couldn't help but wonder where her life was headed. All she seemed to do was work.

It was late on a Friday when Stella trudged home exhausted from the Prichard family's gated mansion. The prospect of going home for the weekend should have been joyful, but instead it brought to mind her resentment of how hard she worked and how her sisters did as little around the house as they could get away with.

Stella perked up as she saw 9-year old Mona running to meet her. Their arms joined in a loving embrace. As the oldest daughter, she regarded herself as Mona's second mother. The precocious child could be rebellious at times.

"What are you eating, Mona?"

"An apple that Cousin Annie Mae threw over the back fence."

Cousin Annie Mae had apple trees in her back yard. Fortunately a limb from one of the trees extended into the Randall yard and provided a brief period of apple picking for the children, unbeknownst to the tree's owner. They referred to this as "throwing over the fence."

Stella felt a pang of disgust as she heard Annie Mae's name. She remembered an incident when this particular cousin had spit on their wooden kitchen floor. Even relatives had little regard for their poorer kinfolk.

"Cuz Annie Mae, why did you spit on the floor?"

"The fish bone got stuck in my throat and there was no napkin to spit it in."

Later, Stella had asked her mother why she tolerated this disrespect from her distant cousins.

"Cousin Henry is a highly respected Republican who can help us. I don't want to turn them away." The children's distinct impression was that Henry was somewhat unsavory in his political dealings and that Madeline felt uncomfortable about being beholden to him. Yet in her mind, the family's well-being required it. So she swallowed her pride.

Stella brought her thoughts back to the present. She asked Mona, "Have you had dinner yet?" The answer was no. Already tired, the answer made Stella angry. She envisioned her sisters in their bedrooms: Laura sleeping; Dimetra pretending to study; Erica, engaged in imaginary adventures with the characters in her books.

A moment later Stella burst into their bedroom and found Laura fast asleep, just as she had assumed. Her anger flared. "It's nearly 6 pm and Mona has had no dinner?" Laura sat up fitfully in bed. It was obvious that she had been awakened from a deep sleep.

"Uhh...I couldn't find anything to cook." Although Laura hadn't thought about dinner until now, some excuse was necessary to save her from Stella's anger. But the explanation didn't calm her older sister.

"You're lying Laura. Momma always has meals planned for us on the weekends. By the way, where is Momma?"

"She's probably asleep. She said that she wasn't feeling too well earlier today."

"If that's the case, she probably feels worse for going without food most of the day," Stella shot back.

As she placed her feet on the floor, Laura thought "*Maybe I did forget about Momma but was that enough reason for you to barge in on me this way?*"

Stella stormed angrily into the kitchen and got some neck bones from the refrigerator. She surmised that dinner would be ready by 7:30 – if the wood for the stove was not too damp to burn.

She ignored Laura who had begun snapping the beans. By this time the household was aroused. Dimetra came in to shuck corn from the garden. Still no sign of Erica, who was undoubtedly engrossed in her most recent book, *The Romance of Tuber Frank.*

By now Stella was writhing with anger. She hated being seized by such moods, yet was powerless to protect herself against them. While the folks at church commented on her charming personality and beautiful smile, her family and close friends regarded her as hard to live with. How many nights had she cried herself to sleep after having pierced her mother's heart with cruel and thoughtless words? But once riled, she couldn't seem to help herself.

Most of all, Stella worried that maybe Madeline was right about her being "marked" by the same mental illness which had plagued Josiah's younger brother. Madeline would tell them stories about Uncle Jake sprawled all over the family home where Josiah took her to live as a young bride. Madeline told and retold how he had once raised an axe over her head. Even worse was Jake's ultimate fate. He had gotten too close to the kitchen fire and his clothes had blazed up, burning most of his body. He had screamed in agony during the long trek by horse and buggy to the "colored only" hospital. Without the family's knowledge, the hospital discharged him to a mental institution, where he died. It was months before the family was told of his death, and they never learned the exact circumstances. From beginning to end, Jake's story gave Stella and the others reason to shudder.

Now striving for a more pleasant demeanor, Stella left the kitchen with a cup of hot tea for her mother. Madeline was sitting up in bed reading a love story which she probably found in Erica's room. Madeline read everything she could get her hands on, especially worn magazines and used books that her employer would pass on to her.

"Momma, I brought you some tea. How are you feeling?"

"Better than I did earlier today. My heart was racing so fast that I got into bed hoping to slow it down."

"Momma, why didn't you get one of the girls to call the ambulance to take you to the hospital?" The ambulance was a little red car, and its appearance at the house would frighten them all. After one emergency trip, Madeline's belching was diagnosed as angina pectoris. It caused heart pain of short duration which caused intense anxiety for everyone.

Madeline answered, "I'm so tired of going back and forth to the hospital. I'm only 38. Do I have to look forward to this the rest of my life?"
Poor Madeline! Feelings of love and compassion filled

Stella at that moment. She embraced her mother once again. "Momma, you know the Lord. Trust him to take care of you."

Stella thought to herself, *"Lord, I'm telling Momma to trust you, yet how I struggle to trust you myself. It seems like I take on another burden as soon as one is lifted."*

Dinner was ready earlier than expected. Dimetra brought a tray of neck bones, rice, corn and string beans into Madeline's room. Stella hastily left to have dinner with Mona.

The weekend went by quickly. On Monday, returning to the Prichard mansion, Stella was surprised to see an attractive young man working in the yard. He had already gotten dirt on the new jeans he had evidently purchased for the new job. There was a sparkle of gray in his brown eyes.

Even a strong fence has gaps. This one was named Justin.

# Chapter Four

## UNFENCING THE RANDALLS

*JUSTIN HAD BEEN HIRED BY* the Prichards to build an archway into their rose garden. Stella was astonished at his boldness and familiarity in approaching her.

"What's your name?" he inquired. Timidly she responded, "My name is Stella Randall. I am the Pritchard's housekeeper."

As she moved to go inside, Justin wanted to draw out the conversation a bit longer. "They seem like nice people," he said.

Stella inwardly reflected that maybe he felt that way since they had given him a job. For herself, she didn't consider the Prichards to be either nice or otherwise. All she was sure of was that the work kept her on her feet all day and the two young Prichard boys were difficult to handle. Although the job served to add a small increase to the Randall family "piggybank," it sapped her energy and robbed her of normal life experiences and adventures for a girl her age.

"What time are you through working at night?" Justin asked.

He was getting even bolder in his approach. *Whoa! I just met you! What business do you have in asking about my work schedule?* Stella thought to herself. But she answered his question. "After dinner. Or whenever I've cleared away the dishes."

Justin grinned. "Maybe we can take a spin in the countryside on one of your free nights?"

Stella hesitated. She had just met this man and he was already making plans to see her again. Yet the thought of being alone with him pleased her more than she was willing to admit. Her thoughts whirled as she considered what Madeline's reaction would be. *Me? Taking a spin with him in his car? Momma, I know you don't want to hear that!*

"We'll talk about it later. I have to go now," she said, turning and walking up the driveway without a backward glance.

Their friendship developed quickly. Justin would come to the back door for water and Stella added cookies or ice cream to the tray. For the next six months they chatted about everything and nothing. Just being in his company was a balm of delight to Stella's spirits.

She was pleased when Justin came over one night as she was getting ready to prepare for bed. "It's such a beautiful night – there is a new moon and the stars are dancing. I wonder if we could go out for a ride in my Ford Model T."

Delighted, Stella quickly followed Justin to his car.

The evening was a turning point. After a childhood and youth of tight supervision, followed by constant and tiring work in early adulthood, Stella was more than ready to have a social life and dabble with romance. Justin brought her flowers that he hid in the car until the pair managed to slip away after their chores were completed. He kissed her on the cheek as he helped her into his car.

Stella nearly toppled over the vase with the six red roses

on the floor beneath her seat. "Oh Justin, are these for me? She picked up the vase quickly and cuddled it to her breast.

"I was hoping that you would like them. They remind me of you, always in a state of peace and calm."

*Dear God, please don't ever let me have a temper tantrum with him. I believe that I am in love with him. But then I'll probably never have a need to find anything wrong with Justin. He's so caring! My wish is his command.*

Poor Stella. She nearly lost her temper with Justin the very next day when he came in to work with lipstick on his cheek.

"Justin! You're rushing in here late with lipstick all over your face. Where did you sleep last night?"

Justin was shaken by her outburst. Why should Stella show concern over his lateness? And Anna only kissed me on my right cheek.

"My sister, Anna, was having last minute problems with her car so I had to drive her to her job. So I received a quick peck for being a good scout".

Stella shuddered inwardly with fear. *Dear Lord, please remove this deep anger and jealousy from me. Please teach me to reason before I speak.*

"I'm so sorry, Justin. I had no rights to berate you. Would you please forgive me?" This incident precipitated their first passionate embrace.

Justin reserved a table at the *Pour Vous* restaurant for a late dinner after work. They were seated in a choice area which allowed them to observe the sailboats on Campano Bay. Stella was ecstatic with joy. Never in her wildest dreams had she imagined herself in such a moment!

She hesitated when Justin reached for her hand to lead her to the dance floor, remembering her mother's warnings that dancing was an invention of the devil. Yet the thought of being in Justin's arms erased all guilt from her mind. Justin pressed his lips close to her cheek as they moved slowly around the floor. With her own lack of dancing experience, it pleased her to realize that Justin was not very good at mastering the art himself.

Later, Stella threw all caution to the wind as she and Justin spent half the night making love in the Model T. If only time would stand still!

***

While Stella was finding romance, Laura longed for excitement in her life. "School is so boring. What is the point of me going anyway? My teachers don't seem to care whether I get it or not. I'm already 17 in the 11th grade," she fumed.

Her thoughts moved to other complaints. *I live in a crowded, 'rain-bucket' house. And as if we weren't cramped enough, now Aunt Callie and Uncle Miles are living with us in the new room Poppa built off the dining room. And that roof leaks too!*

If there was any way her family was rich, thought Laura, it was in their supply of tin buckets and tubs. They used them for baths, washing clothes, carrying food, watering the garden, and of course, catching rain.

In her mind, Laura ticked off other reasons to resent the houseguests. *Why does Aunt Callie always take more than her share of the cornbread at dinnertime? Her excuse, that she's a slow eater and only fills her plate once, doesn't fly. There is never enough food for the rest of us, especially the kids who have to eat last.*

Laura's frustration turned to her father. *Poppa, he hates to see us have any fun. But at least, sometimes, he treats me better than my sisters, especially Dimetra. Is that because I look the most like him with my golden high cheekbones and full lips? I know I'm the prettiest girl of the family, everybody says so! But even still, when I see that twitch in Poppa's eye, I know I'm not gonna get any special treatment.*

Frustrated at home and school, Laura's urging adolescent hormones caused her thoughts to drift to Horace Grimes. He lived in the government housing projects down the hill. She had met Horace on one of the ferry cruises her family went on once a year. Now that she was 17, her mother allowed her to go to the movies with him--of course chaperoned by her older sister.

How his touch thrilled her! She told her sisters that it caused her blood to race up and down her spine like hot wine! (They wondered how a Randall girl knew about wine of any temperature.) Impatience with school, frustration at home and warm reactions to Horace combined in a fateful decision. Two months later Laura married Horace.

*** 

A few months after meeting Justin, Stella had approached Madeline with trepidation. "Momma, I'm pregnant," she confessed.

"Oh my God, no!" You can't be! I've never even seen you with a man."

"I know, Momma, I didn't tell you about Justin 'cause I was afraid that you would make me stop seeing him."

"Who is this Justin and where did you meet him?"

"His full name is Justin Williams. He's the landscape designer for Ms. Prichard. He was hired a few months ago."

"Tell me", Madeline moaned, "How do you do your job and spend time with this Justin?

"We've been meeting in the evening after our work was done. We took rides in his Ford".

Madeline's heart sank and her spirit deflated. How many times had she told her girls to stay away from men's cars? This was what she had fought so hard to prevent. At 19 years of age her eldest daughter was pregnant. What would relatives and neighbors say? They've long predicted that the Randall girls would create a baby nursery. Madeline remembered her own mother's prediction - "as the first goes, so goes the rest". While Madeline was buried in her personal pain, Stella slipped away quietly.

That night Madeline prayed with deep groaning, "Father, I don't know what to do. I need your help, Lord. I won't be able to face my family and neighbors when this story gets out. And Lord, I have four other daughters to raise. Father God, please make a way out of no way. Thank you Lord Jesus. Amen."

Amazingly, she fell asleep peacefully right away after she finished communing with God.

For before-marriage pregnancies, "shotgun" weddings were an absolute requirement in those days. Madeline met with Justin's mother, Ms. Townsend, a week later. Ms. Townsend lived in a nicer area of the city than the Randalls. She greeted Madeline with a sour face. It was obvious from her attitude that she thought it was Stella's fault that they were in this situation.

Madeline politely listened to her ranting until she calmed down. The wedding was arranged for the next Saturday – for family only. Justin's father was not in the picture, having left Justin's mother for another woman when Justin was six years old. Justin told Stella he believed that

that was the day his mother became bitter and difficult to live with – and had remained so.

On the night of the wedding, Justin took Stella to his mother's house. This is where they would live. For the first time, Stella realized this is where Justin had always lived.

Their son Charles was born five months later – nearly eight weeks early. The premature birth resulted from Stella going into labor after tripping on a clothes line pole and falling. Madeline prayed with thanksgiving that her first grandchild and oldest daughter came through the ordeal in good health, adding a word of gratitude that because injury activated the birth, the time of conception would forever be blurred. No sideways looks or tart remarks from suspicious kinfolk - God was good indeed!

*\*\**

The third daughter, Dimetra, followed a different path. She had always been somewhat apart from the others, caught in "middle child" syndrome. Her two older sisters, Stella and Laura, had been inseparable. Erica, who was two years her junior, preferred living the vicarious life garnered through reading books. Mona, the youngest sibling, was still a child jumping rope.

Adding to Dimetra's differentness, and a source of some distress for her, was the contrast between her family's mixed brown hues and her own ruddy complexion and hair. This frustrated her and sparked "acting out" episodes that set her apart in temperament as well as appearance. She had endless confrontations with her siblings, and her churlish interferences in the lives of those closest to her earned the derisive label of "red headed mule." Dimetra compensated somewhat by directing her attention to the neighborhood children, none of whom would dare to challenge her authority.

With her two older sisters married and gone from the family, Dimetra was the first of the family to graduate from high school. Yet despite a brilliant mind, she was unable to afford higher education. She married Don, her childhood sweetheart, and began a lifelong pursuit of entrepreneurial success. Her position with Kessler Beauty products proved to be a successful venture. Both young and older women flocked around her, enamored with her ability to magically transform them from slavish Cinderellas to beautiful princesses. For some of the younger women, she became a mentor and role model – independent and successful through her own hard work, while others were put off by her outspoken ways. In truth, few were neutral about Dimetra – they either liked her strongly or disliked her intensely. Her sisters recognized the extremes, which always depended on Dimetra's mood of the moment.

***

The older sisters had left the Randall nest at a momentous time, as the Great Depression had taken hold with a vengeance. Harold, now an adolescent, went to work helping neighbors prepare their gardens for spring planting. Unlike his sisters, he had relative freedom to leave the fence, especially to supplement the family income. His pay was just a pittance, and half of it went into the Randall family piggybank. With the rest, he was able to buy a bicycle that he treasured.

One day Harold was mending the bike's broken front wheel when he heard the voice that always made him grimace. "Boy," Josiah called, "bring me some wood from the woodshed. Try to get some small pieces since this wood is too damp to make a fire in the stove."

It enraged Harold that at age 14, his father called him "boy." Sometimes he wondered if Josiah even knew his name. It seemed to Harold that his father spoke to him only to issue a command like "bring me a switch," or "wash your feet." The son could not remember a time when his father showed him any special attention or looked him squarely in the eye.

As he put the bike aside to fetch the wood, Harold

thought to himself, *"Momma always told me that Poppa wanted all boys, and since he doesn't pay attention to my sisters, you might think I'd be the focus of his pleasure. But he doesn't even remember my name! He calls the girls by their names – even the dog Rover! Does anybody around here love anybody else? Is the use of that word forbidden? I know Momma loves me but I don't recall her ever telling me except when I was being punished."*

"I'm beating you because I love you," Madeline would tell her son. "I'm trying to make you a better person."

Thanks to a recent snowstorm, he knew that dry wood would be scarce. However truth be told, he'd rather be outside in the cold than have to freeze indoors and listen to his father's grunts. Among his sisters he felt like a loner, and he and Mona were especially prone to arguments. Throughout their childhood and youth, Harold cared little for his younger sister, not realizing that she was actually only angling for his attention with her ploy of manipulating their father against him.

Erica, on the other hand, seemed to have charmed her brother. Mona noticed the difference. "Harold," she asked, "how come you gave Erica that pretty little talking doll for Christmas and gave me this coloring book?" Harold replied, "It's my money and I do what I please with it. You could have bought a doll for yourself if you hadn't used up your allowance to buy a measly gift for everybody in the family."

Sometimes Mona strongly resented Erica's control over Harold and his seeming dislike for her. At other times she longed to share Erica's magnetic ability to coerce and convince family members of her righteousness. Erica, it seemed to Mona, was a special case to one and all.

# Chapter Five

## MONA GROWING UP

**LIKE THE FENCE AROUND** their house, the Randalls' porch came to hold deep symbolic meaning for Mona. At times it was the center of conflict, but more often it was a place of communion and pleasure. While she and Harold had many differences, at night on the porch, the sister and brother marveled together at the beauty of the night sky, filled with astronomical wonders.

In the summer, the whole family choked and coughed on the porch around a smoldering pot-fire built to keep mosquitoes at bay, enjoying their time together in spite of the smoke. As a teen, Mona entertained her dates on the porch, ever conscious that her mother was paying close attention in the front bedroom. All her life, she would never live anywhere without a porch, and it would forever be her place for retreat and reflection.

In later years, Mona's childhood gave her much to reflect upon – especially the dynamics of Randall family relationships, the rough edge of poverty, and the harsh realities of racial prejudice. Chester was a socially segregated town for the most part, and discrimination was strong. From Madeline, the Randall children heard a constant message – "you are just as good as anybody else." Their mother never wavered from that position, no matter what the circumstances might be.

Yet she couldn't shield her children from experiences with racism. Traveling south on the train to visit family, Mona had tried to enter a small store at one of the stops along the way. She was told she didn't belong there and was hustled outside.

When Mona entered first grade at age 5, she already was a reader, influenced by her five older siblings and her mother's voracious reading habits. Well advanced compared to her classmates, she was soon promoted a grade – which put her in the same class as brother Harold. He wasn't pleased, especially at having to help her with homework.

Mona found elementary school boring. The two teachers were Ms. Jacobs, who also was the principal, and Ms. Peabody. Their standard practice was to hand out worksheets or coloring papers to the students and then chat with each other in the hall while the children did what Mona considered "busy work." Once a little boy named Phillip tried to get Mona's attention by throwing spit balls. She had no interest in Phillip and was annoyed by the spit balls. When she had had enough, she fought with him – which led to a "lashing" with a ruler at school, a note sent home to her parents, and more punishment there.

(Years later, volunteering in a neighborhood public school in Atlanta, Mona saw the same "busy work" pattern being repeated. She organized her own small group within the class to engage the students with personal instruction.)

The unchallenging experience of school continued through her early grades. By the time elementary school was finished, Mona was a prime candidate for dropping out – and the next chapter of her education started on a bad note as well. On the first day at Whitfield Middle School, the principal, Mr. Jackson, startled Mona by asking her what state she lived in. Mona went blank, either not remembering or unsure that she knew.

"Well Mona, I'll have to keep you after school for not preparing your homework," he said. Whitfield was several miles from Reaney Street, and it was dark by the time she got home – yet the incident was a preview of a total change in her thinking and attitude about school. Encouraged by Mr. Jackson, in middle school Mona became an enthusiastic and productive student.

The principal had a passion for training young minds. He tutored Mona nearly every day after school, unaware of the distance she had to walk, or that she and Harold had to pass through belligerent communities and endure racial slurs from classmates, most of them from Polish neighborhoods.

In spite of these difficulties, Mona thrived. Mr. Jackson awakened her to the excitement and potential of the world she would face. She had a special interest in math and history and excelled in these subjects. In middle school, Mona became a confident, avid learner.

Her elementary school had been racially segregated, and in middle school the student body included multiple ethnicities. Advancing to junior high, she was back in a segregated environment. She continued to do well in her studies but had to endure bullying classmates. Most of the girls in her class were much larger than the diminutive

Mona, and the biggest ones picked on her whenever they could. Yet Mona had a protector in one of her teachers, Margaret Darwin. This teacher took a special interest in Mona, even arranging for her to be included in field trips for which the Randalls could not afford to pay.

Other than school, Mona's only "outside the fence" experience as an adolescent was church, which occupied most Sundays. The Randalls were Baptists, and Madeline and Josiah insisted on faithful attendance. The older daughters sang in the choir. Once Harold and Mona were old enough to sit apart from their parents, they occupied "the mourner's bench," a front pew for the not-yet-converted who awaited the moving of the Holy Spirit. Both would have preferred another seating arrangement.

The service itself didn't move young Mona very much. The minister – a known womanizer – would work himself to a "whoopin' and hollerin'" state in an effort to elicit shouting from the congregation. Once safely back home, Mona and her siblings would laugh about his histrionics.

After the lengthy morning service, the Randalls barely had time for a midday meal before the Baptist Young Peoples Unit (BYPU) met. This activity combined recreation and Bible study, which Mona enjoyed. One day, giving her testimony, she expressed the hope to be a missionary –

feeling the urge to be in ministry of some sort. BYPU was a formative experience, and some of the girls she met there remained her lifelong friends.

During the week, while Madeline and Josiah were away at work, Mona and her siblings spent much time on their own – guarded by the fence, of course. Both parents were hard workers, and Josiah was always eager to pick up any available extra job.

Left to their own devices, one of the children's favorite pastimes involved a big black pot that sat in the yard. They would fill it with water, build a fire and experiment cooking different foods, such as boiling corn. Once Mona and Harold snuck into a neighbor's garden and brought back several potatoes to boil. The escapade was witnessed by an unknown tattler who told their parents, and they wound up being punished.

At Christmas Mona and her sisters usually got dime-store dolls which didn't last long. So they made their own dolls by pulling up a certain type of grass that grew in a ditch that ran just outside the yard. When the soil was washed away from the plants, the grass and roots furnished doll hair to braid.

One Christmas, Mona, Harold and Erica received a sled

to share, which they greatly enjoyed in the deep snow that could build up drifts of five feet or more. A sledding accident left Mona with a deep gash in her thigh. She had a safer time with a pair of skates which the three also shared, although she never really learned to skate well.

In warm weather they set up a tennis court in the yard, using equipment that Madeline's employer gave her. Sometimes they played softball or baseball. For an indoor game, they played "flinch 'em" ... until the sound of Josiah's key turning in the front door sent them all scurrying to avoid being put to work.

Mona lived in keen awareness of the danger of fire, because house fires were common in the neighborhood, including the home of several relatives. In the Randall's dining room, there was a ceiling passageway with a pull-down ladder that provided entrance into the attic. She and Harold would pull down the ladder and climb into the attic for fun. In cold weather, sparks from the chimney of the pot-bellied stove in the dining room below would light up the darkness. Mona later considered it a miracle that fire never broke out in the house.

But Mona's greatest childhood fear was for her mother's poor health. Whenever the little red car was summoned to take Madeline to the hospital, Mona doubted that she would come back. Whenever Madeline started breathing deeply, Mona would ask her if she wanted water. Madeline made fun of this until the day when her doctor said that dehydration was part of her problem.

Whatever her state of health might be at any given time, Madeline retained her vigilance over her daughters. She paid close attention to friends they brought home, to make sure they weren't "fast" or "fresh." The older daughters had a friend named Carol whose influence Madeline suspected was not of a positive nature. Away at work in the afternoons when Carol would visit, Madeline instructed Mona to hide under the bed and report to her on the nature of Carol's conversation.

Innocent Mona was not precisely sure what she should be listening for. Even later, in junior high school, she was puzzled when a classmate named Bernice once asked her if she had ever had a man lay on top of her to make her feel good. Oblivious, Mona inquired of Madeline and quickly regretted asking the question. Her mother gave no explanation but ordered her to have nothing more to do with Bernice, whose company Mona enjoyed. How to handle the split with her friend proved a moot point, since Bernice very soon dropped out because of pregnancy.

In these youthful years, it wasn't just Madeline's fence

that kept Mona close to home, with few attachments outside her family. At school it was impossible not to notice that many of her classmates had nicer clothes, and more of them. The Randall girls received only two new outfits apiece to last the entire school year.

Mona's first romantic interest developed during her middle school years. He was curly-headed Earl, who delivered produce from the local market. Whenever their paths would cross, each broke out in a broad grin. But little other than long-distance smiles was possible from behind the fence.

The sting of material lack during those years left its mark on all the Randall girls, and they made up for it later. As adults, all five sisters would be known as sharp dressers, and they competed with each other to outfit their mother in stylish, becoming clothes. Mona thought of it as their way of having "the last word" over bleak childhood memories of doing without. She keenly recalled feeling like the poorest student in class, which had led her to shy away from making friends. "I didn't feel like I had anything to offer," she said many years later.

Yet even so, Madeline's message had taken root and was growing – "You're just as good as anybody."

# Chapter Six

## COUSINS

***ON HER 11TH BIRTHDAY***, Mona felt miserably alone as she stood on the back porch of her family's bungalow. Today was her birthday and no one seemed to care. Mona's family had never shown much enthusiasm in celebrating birthdays, so it was a mystery that she should feel that her eleventh year on earth mattered. She shivered as she gazed at the dark clouds above presenting the ominous threat of rain. It appeared even the weather had conspired with her family in an attempt to make her day miserable.

It was Saturday, and Mona imagined what was taking place inside the house. Her three sisters were making every effort to be busy and stay out of their father's sight. Poppa was about to drop his cigar on the floor as he nodded by the pot-bellied stove. Momma was shut up in her bedroom, engaged in deep prayer and struggling with her ongoing effort to breathe.

As long as Mona could remember, her mother had been in poor health. Wracked with angina pectoris, her frail body often labored to breathe. Her sisters claimed it was because their mother had returned to the cotton fields too soon after the birth of her babies. Yet despite her ailments, Madeline played dodge ball and hopscotch with them, and Mona considered her mother to be brilliant when she helped with homework.

Mona turned quickly at the sound of the opening of the rickety screen door. Stella had come home from working through the week at her live-in job at the Prichard home. Mona ran to embrace her as Stella's falsetto voice rang out: *"Happy birthday to you, happy birthday to you, happy birthday dear Mona... Happy birthday to you!"*

In an instant Mona's pity party turned to joy. Stella pulled a tiny box from her purse and handed it to Mona. *"Oh! A tiny gold ring filled with diamonds!"*

Mona placed the ring on her finger, proud of the gift that undoubtedly came from Woolworth's Department Store.

Stella then proceeded to question Mona concerning every event in her life since they had parted a week ago.

The house came alive when the two of them entered. Their sisters were preparing dinner and Josiah was awake and getting a hasty chew on his tobacco before dinner. Mona knew that her three sisters' sudden business was an attempt to avoid upsetting Stella, all of them afraid of her uncontrollable temper.

This was a birthday Mona would long remember, because it represented a "line in the sand" between childhood innocence and growing awareness.

At age eleven Mona longed to be tall like her sisters with a head-turning figure like Laura's. Mona also envied their hair which grew long and curly, while hers remained short. The sisters coveted Mona's flawless complexion, which would be widely admired as she grew into adulthood.

While Mona was short for her age, there was evidence of her budding maturity. This was noticed by her cousin Stanley, one of the steady stream of family members whom the Depression had brought under the Randall roof for various durations.

First to come was Aunt Callie, who claimed the bedroom

in the recent addition on the back of the house. Madeline's brother Miles took up residence for a while. Then came Stanley. He was Madeline's 22 year old nephew from Georgia and was tall and good looking. In spite of the fact that Mona was only 11, he pressured her for sexual favors, kissing and touching her inappropriately. He warned her not to tell anyone.

Yet Stanley was hardly discreet about his interest, often saying to her in the company of others, "Say the word – I'm ready when you are." If any family member ever asked Stanley what he meant or suggested the inappropriateness of his interest in an 11 year old, Mona never was aware of it. Despite her distaste for Stanley's aggressive advances, she obeyed his orders not to tell her parents or anyone else of his behavior.

Four years later at age 15, Mona had a different reaction to another cousin who moved in. Reuben was Aunt Callie's 20 year old son. For reasons Mona did not know, Reuben walked with a cane. She cared much more about the fact that he had a beautiful tenor voice and sang love songs to her. Thoroughly smitten, she looked on Reuben as a knight in shining armor. He was her first love.

She begged him to take her away, pleading "Even with all

this family, I feel so alone. I just want to be somewhere alone with you."

"But Mona, you're only 15 years old, much too young to leave home."

She protested. "But you're 20 and can get a job so we can be together forever."

Although he told her it was impractical for the two of them to run away, he didn't discourage her advances. Mona believed they were in a romantic relationship that Reuben valued as much as she did.

Then, out of the blue, Mona's world was shattered. Completely unknown to her, Reuben had also been courting Erica. When he approached Madeline to ask to marry Erica, he told her that Mona was pursuing him with pleas to run away. He made no mention of the mutual relationship which he had enjoyed and encouraged. Madeline angrily confronted Mona, called her daughter "a little slut" and accused her of "sneaking around after Reuben in dark corners." Crushed and bewildered by his betrayal, Mona made no denials or explanations, feeling that it was useless. With her heart broken, she resolved never to trust anyone again.

Meanwhile plans for marriage went forward between Erica and Reuben. Accompanied by their parents, they went to a magistrate to perform the ceremony. When the official asked if anyone had reason to object, Aunt Callie surprisingly stood up to protest the wedding because of the family connectedness. Just like that, the nuptials were called off.

Back at Reaney Street, life continued much as before although somewhat awkward. Reuben was gone, but his mother continued to occupy the back bedroom. It would be six more years before Erica married and left with her husband Lee. Mona didn't realize it at the time, but a fissure had come between the two of them that would reappear later in life.

There was one more male live-in cousin for Mona to contend with – her mother's nephew Wayne. Although married, he cornered her and tried to force himself on her, then offered her "good money" if she would consent to sex. She fended him off, yet the experience compounded an impression that had begun with Stanley and intensified with Reuben. Mona became aware that she held a strong attraction to the opposite sex and could lead them on with ease. There was a fine line, it seemed, between innocent flirtation and creating expectations of something more – and she had to walk that line like a graceful dancer.

This was a skill Mona cultivated, one which she would often put to use in her life.

# *Chapter Seven*

## MONA OUT IN THE WORLD

**THE BAFFLING SITUATION WITH** Reuben, Erica and Madeline would linger in Mona's mind for many decades. However from an outsider's perspective, the whole matter seemed to just fade away. Within the Randall family, hard feelings never seemed to be actively resolved. Instead they simmered on the figurative back burner. Sometimes they were simply forgotten in time. At other times they might blaze up into fresh grievances at an unexpected moment.

Madeline never sought to reconcile with Mona over her harsh words in the Reuben matter. In her mind, older folk were always right and need not apologize to a young person. Once he was out of the picture, Erica said nothing about him or her sister's attachment to him. She continued to live at home, working as a stenographer in the office of a neighborhood agency. Looking back years later, Mona would come to think of the episode as "exhibit A" in her family's inability or unwillingness to ask for or offer forgiveness, or to express love openly.

Meanwhile Mona and Harold followed Dimetra as the second and third members of the immediate family to graduate from high school. To the pride and delight of the Randalls, Mona was chosen by the faculty to be valedictorian of the class. When informed of the honor by a teacher, Mona was surprised – she ranked in the top third but did not consider herself an academic stand-out. The faculty thought otherwise. At age 16 she stood in front of the graduation audience and delivered her valedictory speech without a flutter, foreshadowing the considerable public speaking she would do in years to come.

With her high school triumphs still fresh, Mona felt adulthood fast approaching. She became engaged to a young friend named Lawrence. Her mother approved of him, meaning she trusted him to keep Mona chaste. Mona liked him but was hardly swept off her feet. She learned from Lawrence that he dallied with other girls in order to fulfill her mother's trust and not pressure Mona for sex. She felt not the least pang of jealousy and was in no hurry to change their relationship at the altar. The hands-off relationship worked for everyone.

She had ambitions that had nothing to do with marriage. "Momma, can I go to college?" Mona asked Madeline around the time of her high school graduation. Her mother hesitated before replying. "No Mona, there are several reasons. You're only 16 and too young to go out in the world. You've never been anywhere away from the family. Plus, where would the money come from?"

Mona countered, "Maybe I could get a job and take a few classes each semester."

But Madeline was firm. "Even still Baby, I'm afraid to allow you to leave me right now. Maybe when you are a bit older."

Madeline did allow her youngest to take employment as a maid in Ms. Ransom's home in suburban New Jersey. She was paid $1.29 a day for a job that required her presence six out of seven days. The compensation barely covered her bus fare and mandatory contribution to the Randall household. The Ransom family had two young boys, ages seven and five, and Mona wondered if they even knew what the word "no" meant. Hearing it seemed to have no effect on whatever their activities of the moment happened to be.

When Mona took the position, Mrs. Ransom promised that a raise would come in time. But two years later, Mona was making the same salary as when she had started. Desperate to extricate herself from the situation, she concocted a story about needing to have her tonsils removed.

"How long before you can come back to work?" Ms. Ransom asked, showing no concern for Mona's health.

"I don't know at the present time," Mona replied.

"I'll try to hold the job for you as long as I can," said Ms. Ransom. It was the last conversation the two would ever have.

Giving up the job was hardly a problem, because better opportunities were at hand for Mona and her entire family. The world was going to war, and America was drawn in. This meant that at long last, the Depression was ending and the economy was shifting to high gear. Jobs were plentiful – good paying jobs at that. Soon Mona was working at the Naval shipyard five days a week. Better pay and weekends off!

The shipyard job brought more than additional money. Mona also expanded her social circle. Every day she rode the train to and from work with April Martin. She and April became best friends.

"It looks like we're headed in the same direction," said April the first day they met. "Do you work at the Base?"

"Yes I do. My name is Mona."

"Good to meet you, Mona. I'm April."

From that day on, they sat together on the train each day. Soon they were sharing their life's hopes and dreams. Love seemed to be in the air – for everyone but Mona. Over the next two years, April became engaged to a wonderful suitor. Mona's sister Erica also fell in love. Mona was still officially engaged to Lawrence, but she felt no real passion for him. He was on active duty in the Army, and she had no intention of sitting home and pining for a faraway soldier.

April and her sister Nancy knew many boys and arranged for Mona to date some of them. In fact, an unspoken arrangement developed in which she and April simultaneously dated several of the same young men – even on the same night. After work, a fellow would head for the Randall house to spend time with Mona. They would visit on the porch, then part at the fence gate with an embrace.

Madeline, watching unseen from a window, would quiz Mona afterwards. "Did he press himself against you?" Sometimes he had, sometimes not – but in either case he would then be off to take April out on the town, since she had much more freedom than Mona did.

Mona did nothing to discourage the visits, although she never discussed them with April. And she drew the line at sharing April's special friend, later fiancé. She never even flirted with him.

Working at the shipyard offered a haven for meeting men. A young man named Mitchell asked her to the movies, but afterwards wanted more affection than she was willing to give. "I want to wait until I'm married to someone I can love," she told him. Mitchell felt aggrieved. "I take you to the movies and buy you popcorn. Don't you think I deserve something for that?" Mona reacted with pure anger. "You think I owe you my body for 30 cents?" she cried. "What about the hot chocolate and cookies I fix for you when we get home? Do I demand payment for that?"

Just then Madeline burst through the front door, thinking

Mona was being attacked. Mitchell mumbled "good night" and was gone from her life.

She met a medical student named Jimmy who wrote interesting and affectionate letters which she kept in a ribboned box. Then she met Irvin, a shipyard worker at least ten years older than she was. She knew nothing about him except that her knees trembled at the sight of him. He sensed her interest and dampened it with concern that seemed fatherly to her. "Mona, you're a wonderfully gifted young lady," he said. "I feel there is a beautiful life out there waiting for you. I could never forgive myself if I dared to interfere in your future."

As Mona reflected on Irvin's gentle concern for her, she contrasted his integrity with the current unhappy reality of her sister Erica. Mona had overheard a conversation early one morning between Erica and Madeline.

"Momma, I'm quitting Lee. He has been unfaithful to me."

"What happened?" Madeline asked with a tremor in her voice. "How do you know he has been unfaithful?"

"He admitted it! He confessed it!"

Madeline had sat for a long time in silence, and Mona knew her heart was heavy with pain. She could imagine her mother's prayer, *"Father, this is my fourth daughter about to get a divorce. Your word tells me that divorce is wrong. But Lord, how many times have I wanted to leave Josiah? I don't believe he ever loved me. And at this point, I don't have any love left for him. There is fighting and friction between us all the time. What happened to the young man who was so sweet and shy when he approached me and reached for my hand years ago? Worse still, where is that 17 year old girl who was intrigued by his shyness as he gazed into her eyes at the church revival?"*

Erica interrupted Madeline's silence. "Momma?"

Her mother's attention returned. "I'm sorry Erica, my mind drifted. Maybe you should think about this a while longer."

"Why Momma?" Erica cried. "You always told us that we should remain virgins until we were married. I did. Now why should I stay married to a man who disrespects me."

"Well Erica, you know that I don't believe in divorce," Madeline replied.

"Momma, I'm sorry, but I can never live in a relationship like yours and Poppa's, or my sisters."

Madeline was quiet again, knowing that Erica had made up her mind. She sipped the cold cup of coffee in front of her, then excused herself from the table to step outside and water the clematis in the yard.

Erica followed her and continued. "Momma, can you believe what he said when I accused him of infidelity? His excuse was that one of his lady taxi passengers asked him to help her carry groceries to her apartment, and she jumped on him when he came inside! And I asked him, 'You couldn't resist some strange woman who might have every kind of disease imaginable?'"

True to her word, Erica found a condo near the housing development where she worked as a receptionist. Lee came home one night to the home they shared, only to find Erica and the furniture gone.

But living on her own had proved more difficult than Erica imagined, and Mona suspected that she was getting by through the largess of her overly attentive employer.

Given the family tensions that summer, the annual visit from Madeline's sister Lucinda was a welcome break.

Mona had just turned 21, and Lucinda's normally routine stay changed the entire course of her life.

Lucinda always brought provocative tales of the triumphs and successes of cousins back in Georgia. For other members of the family, these stories brought out resentment as they felt their aunt was comparing them unfavorably to their southern relatives. But for Mona, the stories were inspirational. Raised on Madeline's "you're as good as anyone else" mantra, Mona felt herself capable of rising to any standard that these southern cousins might set.

This was especially so because, on a past trip to Georgia, Aunt Lucinda had taken her to visit Gatling College, where Lucinda was taking graduate courses. The college was located in a valley surrounded by tall oaks. Immediately, Mona fell in love with the beauty and calm of the campus. Birds and bees flew leisurely, as it was summer and the students were away. In that atmosphere, Mona came to believe that with some encouragement, all of this could be hers – not just to behold, but to grasp!

Just the right encouragement emerged during Lucinda's visit. Mona shared her hopes for college with her aunt. For Lucinda – a teacher herself – that was all she needed to become Mona's champion.

With amazing speed, and in spite of her mother's misgivings, Mona soon found herself headed south with Lucinda, to fulfill her dreams of college. She was the first in her family to embark on a path of higher education. Mona knew that her life would take a new direction because she was making this choice. With the opportunity to gain a college degree, what kind of world would she create for herself?

# Chapter Eight

## COLLEGE AND ROMANCE

**GATLING COLLEGE WAS ALL** that Mona remembered from her previous visit – beautiful and inspiring. Even more inspiring was the reality of being a college student, with what seemed like an open road of possibilities in front of her.

Mona made friends easily and soon was inducted into the Delta Sigma Theta sorority. However, while her social life was active, she kept a strict focus on why she was at college. Plus, as teachers had discovered in middle and high school, Mona was a natural student with an instinctive curiosity and a persistent desire to understand the world around her.

She was just two months into her freshman year at Gatling when a surprise visitor appeared. It was Madeline, who had come to see for herself if her baby daughter could survive away from home. She stayed with Mona in the dorm, and early one morning before the sun had come up, they were awakened by a knock on Mona's door. It was Cece who lived on the same hall. "Mona, do you have a decent deck of cards I can borrow?" "Uhh, no I don't," Mona answered.

She thought to herself, *What a time for someone to ask me for cards!* All her life she had been taught that playing cards was a vice after the devil's own heart, sure to send a person straight to hell. What bad luck that her mother, the teacher of that lesson, should be in earshot at this particular moment!

Sure enough, Madeline was quick to speak up, "Mona, I can't believe that you play cards after all that I taught you about the evil in card games." Her daughter didn't cave in to the rebuke. "Momma, I don't feel that I'm doing anything wrong or evil when I play a friendly game of cards." That was the end of the conversation, to Mona's surprise and relief.

Later, she learned that one of her cousins, Madeline's favorite nephew, was responsible for her mother's future silence on the subject of cards. Hearing of the episode in the Gatling dorm, he offered Madeline wise advice. "Aunt Madeline, you should thank God every day that Mona is doing nothing worse than playing cards, which is probably nothing more than an enjoyable pastime with her friends."

College life proceeded smoothly and happily that first year until bad news arrived in February from Chester. Mona's friend April Martin was quite ill. April had been planning for her wedding in June. At Mona's urging, Madeline called Mrs. Martin to find out more. Madeline reported to Mona that April's mother confirmed the seriousness of the situation, adding that April's sister Nancy was also sick. But Mrs. Martin had been very vague about the matter, Madeline said.

Mona followed up with her own call to the Martin home and received the same ambiguous, yet dire report. Soon after she learned that April and Nancy had died within a few days of each other. Their bodies were cremated. Mona never heard the cause or circumstances of the mysterious deaths. Reflecting later, she wondered if the sisters had been victims of back-alley abortions.

The loss wracked Mona with pain. She had cared for April and enjoyed her company like no other friend. In her grief she turned to the God that her mother had so often called upon.

*\*\**

Early in her sophomore year, Doug came into Mona's life.

She was meeting her friend Crystal at the college inn. Crystal approached with a young man. "Mona, I want you to meet my homey, Doug," Crystal announced. Mona's heart quickened at the sight of him. "A creamy Adonis," was how she would remember that first glimpse. He was five feet nine inches tall, with curly hair, dreamy eyes and thick lashes. She could hardly catch her breath as Crystal chattered on, giving her more information about Doug.

"He was just discharged from the Army and is coming back to school," Crystal explained. As Mona breathed a hello and reached out to shake his hand, her friend blurted out, "Go on, girl! Why don't you give a returning soldier a big hug!"

Still unable to find her voice, Mona embraced him without hesitation. Later that night she wrote a letter to her sister Erica telling her she had found the man she wanted to marry. Erica replied with two words, "Get him!"

The strong attraction was mutual. Doug was just as drawn to Mona as she was to him. They took advantage of every opportunity to spend time together, even sharing their meager food allowances at Gatling's tiny snack shop that could seat only ten patrons at a time.

He finally noticed her engagement ring. "That's a nice diamond ring on your finger," he said. "Are you engaged?"

Mona berated herself silently for not having removed the ring when she first met Doug. She confessed, "Yes, I'm engaged. My fiancé is serving in the Army."

His response was a silent frown, but nothing spoken. Mona wanted to tell him that the ring no longer mattered to her, that her relationship with Lawrence couldn't compare with the feelings forming between the two of them. She wanted to scream at the top of her lungs, "I've already decided you are the man I intend to marry!"

But how could she possibly say such a thing? She feared looking desperate, and also of frightening Doug away by seeming uncommitted to him by wearing another man's ring. Yet by saying nothing, she discouraged his interest. Doug was a man of honor, and from that point he began to drift away from her.

One of Mona's roommates, Corinne, began to date Doug. It broke Mona's heart to see them together at dances and social gatherings. At night Corinne would whisper to Anna, a third roommate, about highlights of their dates, just loud enough for Mona to hear. It seemed that back in his hometown, Doug had left a girl named Daphne and might still be carrying a torch for her. Mona wondered if learning about her own engagement had prompted Doug to think of his relationship with Daphne as unfinished business.

Mona determined that she must take quick action. She devised a strategy to recapture his interest by appearing aloof. She made a point of showing up anywhere he might be present, like the tennis court, then taking no notice of him. She even began rising at 6 a.m. three days a week to go to the track and run, knowing he would be there, and also that she would never be a track star.

Hoping that he had strong feelings for her, she wanted his attention again – all of it! So she gave him none of her own, steering clear of direct contact, refusing to join him in stimulating discussions in class or at the college inn, with the intent of drawing him out. Her strategy worked!

"Mona, what's wrong?  Are you angry with me?" he asked one day.

"No," she replied.  "Why should I be angry with you?"

"I just wondered why you don't join in class discussions. And I miss sharing meals at the college inn," he answered.

"It's just that I've been kind of busy lately," she said demurely.

To herself, she thought – *What a lie!  How many days and nights have I fretted over missing Doug in my life? I know without a doubt that I'm in love with him.  It's the only reason I'm trying to be cool, when I know that I long to be cuddled in his arms.*

Mona knew the aloof approach was working when she began receiving letters from Doug.  In these messages he took responsibility for the brokenness of their friendship. Progressively, the letters became more passionate.  He described Mona as an angelic being that he had foolishly displeased.  She treasured these declarations of love and felt sure he was leading up to a marriage proposal.

Near the end of the school year, the two of them were given leading roles in a romantic play.  Their first kiss was on the stage – yet it could not have been more genuine. Each had found the heart of a lifelong companion, even to eternity.

They were sharing peanut butter crackers in the snack shop when Doug sighed, "I guess this is goodbye, since you'll be going home to marry that guy."

"At this point I don't know what to do," she said. "But what I do know is that I don't want to get married before we can figure out where this relationship is headed."

Doug grimaced. "I can't bear the thought of losing you. I wonder – could I go with you to your home?"

"Why not?" Mona's voice rang with excitement. "We could at least give our love a try."

Relaxing on the northbound train, Doug confided to her, "My cousin Jake got married at nineteen, even after I begged him to wait 'til he was older." Mona didn't respond, lost in her own thoughts. It had been a year since she was in Chester, and she was deeply anticipating the family reunion. Yet there was reluctance in her return. She was sure that little had changed in her home or neighborhood. She thought of her recurring nightmare of the stove in the dining room exploding.

"Mona, I've lost you," said Doug. "You are so deep in thought."

"I'm sorry Doug," she answered. "I was drifting into childhood memories."

He returned to the subject of his cousin Jake's early marriage. "What's wrong with him getting married?" Mona asked.

"Why would he marry at such a young age?" Doug asked. "Why not?" she retorted. "Where's the fun in growing old alone, nobody to keep you warm, no children or grandchildren to hold in your arms?"

Doug's eyes lit up as a broad smile covered his face. "Mona, will you marry me?"

At last! Mona's heart leaped for joy. Gazing deeply into Doug's eyes, she replied, "Yes Doug. I would love to be your wife."

The "welcome home" to Reaney Street was awkward, as Lawrence was there to greet her. No one in the family had prepared him with the news of a new man in Mona's life. She offered him back his ring, which he refused to take. He left, understandably hurt and angry.

The following morning, Mona and Doug joined Madeline in front of the fireplace. Mona was delighted at Doug's ease with her mother and the rapport the two quickly established. "You'll need to take a firm hand with her, she's always been spoiled," Madeline advised him.

Ten days later, Mona and Doug were joined in marriage in front of that same fireplace, surrounded by approving family members who looked on fondly. Mrs. Mona Cartwright! It didn't matter that Doug's mother (whom Mona had not yet met) sent her a wedding ring from the dime store Woolworths, or that Mona wore her cousin Val's wedding dress, or that her mother struggled to give them one hundred dollars for the honeymoon. She was married to the man of her dreams.

# *Chapter Nine*

## MARRIAGE

**"ENTREAT ME NOT TO** leave thee, or to return from following after thee for whither thou goest, I will go, and where thou lodgest, I will lodge. Thy people shall be my people, and thy God, my God. Where thou diest, I will die, and there will I be buried. The Lord do so to me and more also, if ought but death part you and me."

Doug first spoke the words of Ruth 1:16-17 to Mona on their wedding day. For many years afterwards on her birthday or their anniversary, he would begin his devotions with either that passage or lines from E. B. Browning –

*How do I love thee? Let me count the ways.*
*I love thee to the depth and breadth and height*
*My soul can reach, when feeling out of sight*
*For the ends of being and ideal grace.*
*I love thee to the level of every day's*
*Most quiet need, by sun and candle-light.*
*I love thee freely as men strive for right.*
*I love thee purely as they turn from praise.*
*I love thee with the passion to put to use*
*In my old griefs and with my childhood's faith.*
*I love thee with the love that I seemed to lose*
*With my lost saints. I love thee with the breath,*
*Smiles, tears, of all my life; and if God choose,*
*I shall love thee better after death.*

Their wedding night was spent in the very bedroom on Reaney Street where Mona had slept all her life until leaving for college. Memories flooded of how Stella and Laura had cuddled their baby sister until too much tossing and turning caused them to push her out of bed. No problem now, as she and Doug needed so little space.

Madeline's one hundred dollar gift allowed the newlyweds to spend a week at an Atlantic City guesthouse. Mona never left the room the whole blissful week, and Doug went out only to bring back sandwiches and drinks. They could not get enough of each other.

Following the honeymoon, Mona and Doug returned to Gatling for their junior year, moving into a one bedroom apartment with a tin roof which had once housed Army recruits. Both of them found work on campus – Doug in the dining room and Mona as a file clerk in the administration building. It was their "life is a bowl of cherries" time – yet there were also worrisome foreshadowings.

The first involved his career. A political science major, he was interested in a diplomatic career with an eye on one day being an ambassador to an African nation. So Mona was greatly surprised when in that last year of school, he raised the idea of becoming a clergyman.

Although he sought her reaction to the idea, the times were such that a wife followed the course set by her husband – especially if he felt led to a career of religious service. Yet Mona was aware of the turn this would mean in her own life. To be a minister's wife was to assume a role almost as strictly defined as his own. Plus, their religious upbringings had been starkly different. Doug had been brought up an Episcopalian. The rituals and formality of the Episcopal Church were the polar opposite of the free-form Baptist worship that Mona had always known. She had often accompanied him to a small Episcopal congregation near the Gatling campus and felt a lack of passion in the liturgy and worship experience. Along with the career change surprise, Mona was saddened that the sensual relationship of their honeymoon already had begun to ebb. Doug often expressed his love for her, but his libido was low and their love making left her unsatisfied. She imagined experiences that lifted her to ecstasy, which he could no longer provide.

Most of her concern centered around his jealousy. Initially she mistook it for passion. When Mona first noticed Doug peeking at her through the window of Dr. Miles' sociology classroom, she felt delight at the thought that he loved her so much, he couldn't bear to be separated even for the length of a classroom period. However, eventually the constant peeking became a point of disturbance for both Dr. Miles and herself. Later she would remember this as a harbinger of trouble and wished that early on, she could have intercepted the cruel wounds that his mistrustfulness and controlling impulses held in store for both of them.

One particular episode revealed to her the extent of his obsession. It happened as they were settling into their new apartment in Evanston Illinois, where Doug would attend seminary. The summer they married, Mona had shown him a ribboned box in which she kept mementoes. If he paid much attention to the contents, she couldn't tell it at the time. Now she searched for the box and asked Doug if he had seen it. "I burned it," he replied.

Mona was shocked. "Why Doug, those letters and pictures were my treasures from my growing up years!"

"I wasn't part of them," was his comeback.

"What do you mean?" she asked in anger. "I had a life before we met. You are included in the most important part of my entire life, marriage and a family."

Doug was silent. He had a way of closing down an unfinished conversation that Mona found disturbing. Her mind flashed back to "peeking" episodes in sociology class at Gatling. She sensed an impending fracture in their relationship.

This feeling intensified when Mona met his mother, to whom she took an immediate liking. Elizabeth had reared Doug and his younger brother alone, and Doug never knew his father. Elizabeth was openly partial to the younger son and showed less warmth toward Doug. Mona could see the pain this caused her husband and recognized that it had weighed heavily on him since childhood. While judgmental of Elizabeth for this treatment of Doug, Mona also felt sympathy that her mother-in-law's life had been filled with hardship and disappointments.

In time, other Cartwright family members would share history of the troubled mother-son relationship. It was clear to Mona that Doug had felt unloved and abandoned. Yet while knowing more about Doug's growing up years and family life enlarged her understanding, it did not make Mona's life easier. Increasingly his jealousy was evident. Even a casual conversation or smile with a male acquaintance caused suspicion, and escalated to bitter accusations.

One night as she slept, he hit her hard on the backside. "Doug, why did you smack me on the rump?" she asked.

"You were moving around too much in your sleep," he said. "I know that you were imagining having sex with somebody."

"How can you expect me to rest in peace when you keep me up all hours of the night drinking coffee and trying to convince you that you're the only man in my life?" she retorted.

Doug was having none of it. "Mona, you're lying. I saw the way that you were laughing with Joe last night."

Marsha and Joe had rented the army shelter apartment next to Mona and Doug at Gatling, and they had become close friends of the Cartwrights. They had dropped by often to visit.

"You know what a joker Joe is," she answered. The angry conversation ended, and Mona made every effort to stay awake the rest of the night to avoid a repeat of the ugly scene.

Mona was coming to realize what those classroom "peeking" sessions had really been about – Doug harbored crippling doubt that he could trust her, and felt a compulsion to have her constantly in his sight. Through his need to control her every move, he was reliving the emotional trauma of a childhood without love. Time was not easing his fears, but seemed instead to strengthen them. Mona silently blamed Doug's mother for his insecurities, but she knew that they were now her own to deal with.

As the days passed and Doug's jealousy was increasingly evident, a verse from Song of Solomon was often on Mona's mind. *"Jealousy is as cruel as Sheol. Its flashes are the flashes of fire." (S of S 8:6)*

She turned to prayer. "Lord help me. How can I possibly

deal with this evil enemy called jealousy? Is there no way out of its torment? He tries to bribe my friends to spy on me. He puts paper in the door cracks so he can tell if I've left the house. He's even started pushing me around. I felt mortal fear last week when he tried to drive the car into the river. But I can't tell Momma about this ugly situation. Who can I tell?"

# *Chapter Ten*

## JOYS AND CHALLENGES

*MONA HOPED THAT IN* Evanston, making new friends, Doug's jealous ways would fade. In this she was disappointed. He showed no interest in developing friends among the Seminary faculty or his classmates. Cecil Oxford, a white member of the faculty, made an effort to reach out. One day after class he said to Doug, "My wife Rose and I are having a few folks over tomorrow night for drinks and dinner. We would love for you and Mona to join us."

"I'll see if she's free," Doug answered. "My wife works with a ceramics group on Wednesdays. I'll see if we can make it." He never mentioned the invitation to Mona, although she learned about it from others who had been present. As time went on, the couple would not participate in any social activities.

In Evanston Mona found a job as a receptionist in a doctor's office; however, she soon became pregnant and quit the job. She spent her time making dresses to wear as she waited for the child to be born.

In the last few months of her pregnancy, Doug sent Mona to her parents' home in Chester, as they had decided the baby should be born there. Mona spent much of her time working in the small country store her parents had built on the edge of their lot. It had an eclectic inventory, from food to housewares to oddities. Stella and Laura also worked there at times, along with a cousin, Cynthia, the latest relative to take up residence in the Randall household.

Madeline and Josiah's children were pleased with their parents' entrepreneurial venture. Domestic work over many years had taken a toll on Madeline's fragile health and stamina. The store was hard work, too, but that didn't seem to bother either parent. Having their own business energized them.

In the neighborhood, the store was an instant hit – not only for its convenience but because the Randalls were generous proprietors. In Josiah's case, he simply couldn't count the money correctly to make change. (Madeline and the children tried to make sure he was never there alone to be taken advantage of.) In Madeline's case, she had a natural empathy for the needs of her neighbors. If a young mother came asking for milk for her baby and lacked means to pay, Madeline didn't question the need. Such situations occurred often, and rarely did anyone come back later to make good on payment.

One evening after dark, Mona was closing up the store when she heard a noise and discovered a boy hiding in the shadows. He was waiting until everyone was gone to steal what he wanted and be gone. She recognized him as a local youth as he pushed past her and ran out the door. The episode became common knowledge in the neighborhood, along with the boy's threat against Mona that he was going to "cut that baby out of her." Mona thought little of the threat, knowing that the boy was just angry and embarrassed at having his robbery plan thwarted.

Shortly before Mona gave birth, Doug came to Chester. Mona had once set her mind on having six sons, but when daughter Miriam was born, the young mother thought she was the most beautiful baby in the world.
Doug was now a seminary graduate. The diocese assigned

him to an apprentice position in Philadelphia, which he would hold for three years as he learned the role of a parish priest.

A few months after giving birth, Mona got a job as a social worker, visiting the homes of single women with dependent children each month to verify their eligibility to continue on public assistance. In the public housing projects she began to see things that had never been visible in her sheltered childhood and youth behind the fence. Life there was bleak, and clients didn't welcome Mona's questioning visits. Any hint that continuation of benefits might be in jeopardy was greeted with fury that truly frightened her. Meanwhile, she was under pressure from her supervisors to find grounds for disqualifications that would reduce the welfare rolls. When she didn't produce evidence to terminate enough clients, she was fired.

Losing the job was a huge relief, and not only from the stress of the work. Her sister Laura had cared for baby Miriam while Mona worked, and the child had started calling Laura "Momma." This deeply disturbed Mona, so she was delighted to reassume her caretaking role. Doug took a second job in construction to make up for the income loss, which paid overtime and more than covered the lost wages of her former employment.

By the time another child was on the way, Doug had finished his apprenticeship and gotten his own pastoral charge. He was assigned to an inner-city Baltimore parish which was faltering. The mainly white worshipers had moved from the neighborhood, and the church had not connected especially well with the community's African American newcomers. Here Doug showed what would become his greatest strength as a minister – building up vibrant congregations either from scratch, or from the remains of a failing church.

Mona would later look back on these years as the happiest of her marriage. Son Adam was born four years after Miriam. As the baby lay on her breast, she thanked God for him. He had hardly whimpered during birth – a great contrast to the birth of Priscilla four years later, who pitched a fit as if annoyed that her nesting place had been disturbed.

Mona's parents often came to visit them in Baltimore and were popular with Doug's parishioners. Stella, Laura and Dimetra were aghast at the idea of their rough-hewn father mingling with Doug's parishioners, many of whom were upscale, well educated professionals. Josiah might not be able to read or write, and he might tell stories that embarrassed his daughters, but he was an instant hit at the church. Members embraced his authenticity and honored the fact that he had provided for a family of six children without buckling under to the disadvantages into which he had been born.

Doug convinced Mona to stay at home with the children until they reached school age. Although delighted to be a fulltime parent and homemaker, she felt unfulfilled once the children were in bed for the night. One reason was Doug's inability to meet her sexual needs or her expectations of marital intimacy. Her husband offered little company, having fallen into the habit of coming home at night, turning on the TV and falling asleep. Yet even as she remained unsatisfied in their bedroom trysts, Mona never questioned his love for her.

"Mona," he said, "sometimes I feel that I love you more than ..." "Don't say it!" she broke in. "Never say that! Remember we have a jealous God."

The work to rebuild the parish was proving fruitful. Doug's good looks and charm attracted new members, many of them women. Some of the women were more interested in the pastor than God and made their interest fairly obvious. While Mona noticed and frowned on their boldness, she never felt any qualms that Doug might be moved by their attentions. And he wasn't. What did move him, however, was any attention paid to her by another man. His suspicion and distrust became a constant cloud over their marriage.

They had been in Baltimore several years when an innocent situation with a neighbor reminded her how suddenly and sharply Doug's jealousy could erupt. Having never driven a car before, Mona set out to learn. Doug agreed that she should ask Dexter, their recently widowed friend who lived across the street, to teach her. For two weeks, each weekday morning Dexter took Mona to a nearby driving range to practice behind the wheel. When they had completed the course and Mona was ready for Dexter to take her to the Department of Motor Vehicles to get her license, Doug became strangely belligerent.

"No, you can't go out this morning with that man," he insisted.

"Why not, Doug? Why are you telling me this just as I'm on my way to take my driving test?"

"Because I know you're having an affair!" he answered aggressively.

Angered by the accusation, Mona replied, "'That man' as you call him is named Dexter. He lives across the street.

I thought you two were friends. Why are you making these accusations?"

Doug answered, "Every morning you take a shower and put on perfume before you go out." Evidently Doug had not noticed that she did the same thing before going to church or any outings.

She was resolute, "I'm going to take my driving test, Doug. I've gone too far with this to give up on it now."

His anger turned to pleading that she not go. Mona ignored him, slamming the door behind her as she saw Dexter crossing the street. If her upset state of mind was apparent to Dexter, he made no mention of it. They went to the DMV, and she passed the test.

In Mona's mind, this incident was a threshold moment in the fracturing of their relationship due to Doug's irrational jealousy. There had been earlier indicators but this was a new and frightening low point.

For Doug, the self-inflicted pain of jealous rage was compounded by Mona's seeming lack of sympathy for his feelings. Knowing that she had given him no reason to doubt her fidelity, her resentment compounded with each of his outbursts. She failed to grasp the pain he felt and drifted further away from him emotionally. Her refusal to show understanding or compassion confirmed him in his gloomy imaginings. Both of them realized that a chasm was developing that could not easily be bridged. Neither was open to heeding God's decree that "love beareth all things, believeth all things, hopeth all things, endureth all things." (1st Cor 13:7)

Over ten years Doug had done wonders to build up the Baltimore parish, but his jealous obsessions had started to take a toll on his work. Noting a drop in enthusiasm and convinced of Doug's talents, Bishop Allen proposed a change of scenery to revive his energy.

"Doug, I believe you've been working too hard. It's time for a break from parish leadership. How would you and the family like to take a year in England, for you to study at the Canterbury Cathedral?" Doug reluctantly agreed, praying the new situation would break the constant pains he was enduring in his marriage.

Mona was thrilled at the prospect. She, too, hoped for a healthy disruption in the pattern of Doug's jealous habits. She also recognized the offer as a confirmation of the Church's high regard for Doug's potential and eagerness to advance his career. Excited by the idea of living abroad, she was confident that the children were at a good age for the change – young enough to adjust well and old enough to learn from it.  A new home, fresh experiences, time for travel, the chance to heal their marriage – all in all, the offer seemed heaven-sent.  In what appeared to be a remarkably short time, the Cartwrights were on the high seas.

# Chapter Eleven

## ENGLAND

**SITTING ON THE DECK OF** the enormous Queen Mary, Mona was lost in thought and failed to hear 9-year old Miriam next to her until her daughter tapped her shoulder. "Mommy, how long are we going to be in England?" Mona roused out of her thoughts and answered, "I believe we will be there for about a year." Satisfied, Miriam drifted into her own world of imagination and stared into the expanse of sky.

Mona felt that she could read her daughter's thoughts, anticipating a new adventure with genuine excitement. Five year old Adam, seated at Mona's left, was gazing over the vast North Atlantic waters through glasses he had worn since age two. Priscilla, barely a year old, had been taken to the ship's nursery by one of the stewards.

The first night on board had been delightful. There were after-dinner activities for the children before going to bed. Time alone in a romantic setting had become rare for Mona and Doug, and they took advantage by dancing late into the night. Mona's hopes soared that a renewed bond would be rekindled between them.

But it was not to be. Doug had not confided in the bishop about his marital troubles and now worried that he should have done so. Perhaps this anxiety increased the seasickness that kept him in their cabin for most of the trip. The crew's valiant efforts to mitigate his discomfort were of no avail. Not until the family disembarked did Doug revive. As the family headed for their new home in Dover, he made a quick recovery.

The Cartwrights found a warm welcome in Dover. Three other families from the States were there on seminary assignment, and the Cartwrights quickly connected with them. Bill and Sandra hailed from Alabama. June and Joseph were from New Orleans. The only couple with young children were Philip and Janice, whose two little ones were the same ages as Adam and Priscilla.

There were frequent invitations to tea. The children loved excursions on the train into London, and Miriam and Adam adapted readily to local schools. Doug was asked to preach in several Anglican churches. Mona received invitations to preach and speak to women's groups about the Episcopal church in America. The family also took several trips across the English Channel.

In spite of the good times, Mona's hope for marital serenity was dashed quickly. Their new friend Philip was a natural comedian and at any seminary gathering, he kept everyone in stitches. Everyone except Doug, who resented Mona's enjoyment of the humor. On Thursday nights the seminary couples met for group dinner. Philip and Janice always sought out Mona and Doug to sit at the same table. One evening when Philip was in especially funny form, Mona made an innocent comment – "I really needed these good laughs" – that triggered an angry outburst from Doug when they got home.

"That remark was like inviting him to have an affair," Doug charged. A barrage of distrustful insinuations and outright accusations followed over the next several weeks. Then one night, he arrived at home to accuse her of having slipped away earlier in the day to be with Philip. It was an absurd notion, and she challenged him to explain his reason for thinking so. He refused an explanation but continued accusations until Mona collapsed in tears. "I placed paper in the door, and when I came home it was not there," he finally snapped.

"I opened that door when Janice brought some macaroni and cheese to the children," she threw back at him. "If there was paper, it fell out then."

"You're lying, Mona!" Doug yelled.

This was the last straw for her, and she didn't hold back. "I'm sick and tired of this! I'm sick and tired of you! Just because you can't satisfy me in bed, you accuse me of sleeping with every man I speak to." Doug lunged toward Mona and grabbed her throat in a tight grip, then ran his fingers down her face. The next few seconds were a blur of fear. Somehow she escaped his grasp and ran from the bedroom.

The next day she sought out Janice and confided in her about their desperate situation. Janice put her in touch with a psychiatrist she knew. Doug recognized that he needed help and agreed to see Dr. Hamlin. After only two sessions, Dr. Hamlin advised Mona that he planned to treat Doug with a strong medication that could cause disorientation. He advised her to return to the States while Doug was in treatment.

Two days later, she and the children boarded the Queen Elizabeth for a dreadful voyage to New York. In place of her high hopes during the first passage, she was swamped with fear and doubt about what the future might hold. She and the children went to Reaney Street to stay until Doug's situation clarified. Madeline welcomed them heartily in spite of her surprise. Mona's explanation skirted the real reason for the shortened sabbatical. Although she led her mother to understand there were difficulties in the marriage, Mona portrayed the situation as "normal strife" rather than deep turmoil. She hoped against hope that therapy would bring Doug home in a healing state.

# Chapter Twelve

## MAJOR MOVES

**DOUG RETURNED EIGHT WEEKS** after the family and took up his former charge in Baltimore. It was late winter, and Mona kept the children in Chester to finish the school year rather than move them yet again. For herself, relief at being under her mother's caring wing was another strong incentive to lengthen the visit as long as possible.

When summer came, the family was reunited in Baltimore. Now that the diocese was aware of their problems and Doug's therapy, Mona had thought they might put him in a new assignment with less stress. But she also could see the advantages for him of returning to familiar scenes and people. Doug resumed his pastoral duties with vigor, and his congregation was glad to welcome him back. Still, it didn't take Mona long to realize that the treatment had not produced a lasting change. The jealous impulses were evident, if somewhat more muted. Thankfully, there was no repeat of the physical violence.

As a way to cope with their own emotional distance, both parents turned their energies to the children. They had experienced great disruption in the past year, and now Mona and Doug focused on their successful regrounding back in Baltimore. In parenting, they found common cause and a basis for mutual support. The one thing stronger than Doug's suspicious torment, or Mona's deep unhappiness, was their love for their children and dedication to their well-being.

Mona acknowledged to herself that Doug was a good father, and she regarded herself the same as a mother. As the children grew, Miriam, Adam and Priscilla showed sturdy emotional health without signs of their parents' childhood burdens: Doug's sense of loveless abandonment and Mona's constricted early years behind the Reaney Street fence. The children weren't prone to Mona's pouting or Doug's sulky rage. They showed love freely and didn't hold onto anger. They trusted each other, their parents and the goodness of life.

In school and socially, the children were progressing, and

their distinctive personalities were taking shape. Mona and Doug noticed that Miriam had begun to show signs of restlessness and nervous habits. The family pediatrician advised that as the oldest, too many responsibilities had been placed on her tender shoulders, and she should be encouraged to play more. The strategy worked, and Miriam blossomed into a gifted young girl.

Mona, who had once wanted six boys, watched Adam with special keenness. She was pleased that he had many friends although he didn't strike her as particularly outgoing. Often she thought of how, at his birth, she had cited the 23rd Psalm when he was first placed on her lap and she examined every inch of his tiny body.

The youngest, Priscilla, had ruled the household practically from birth. She had been born at a time when the turmoil between her parents was becoming serious, and her arrival had provided a time of release from Doug's dark imaginings and Mona's mounting frustration. From an early age, Priscilla had a voluble personality and made friends easily. She also was strong willed and prone to mischief. Once when Mona denied her TV privileges because of misconduct, her daughter angrily ran upstairs mumbling, "I hate you." Priscilla was brought up short by her mother's reply, "Right now I don't like you very much either."

Mona became accustomed to getting calls from school about Priscilla's escapades. Answering the phone one day, she recognized the voice on the other end as Mr. Wylie, the principal.

"Mrs. Cartwright, I'm afraid that Priscilla has demonstrated disorderly conduct again. She intentionally dropped a book down three flights of stairs, and one of the teachers was slightly injured. I'm afraid we'll have to suspend her for a few days." Not long afterwards, Priscilla was suspended again for being in the wrong place at the wrong time – attending a fight away from the school involving several other students.

Perhaps Priscilla's school adventures were an unconscious reaction to her awareness of the tension between her parents. Doug's accusations of infidelity had fired up openly once again, and Mona had reached a point of barely bothering to deflect them. She knew that any conversation she had with a man, or any comment she might make about a man, would trigger jealousy. Nothing seemed to break the toxic pattern between them.

A fleeting respite from the tension came on August 28, 1963, when she and Doug went to Washington to join the March on Washington for Jobs and Freedom. They stood on the Mall and heard Dr. Martin Luther King Jr. share his dream for justice and equity in American society. A sublime peace had defined the atmosphere that day, making Mona think of what Heaven must be like. The Cartwrights and many of their friends went forward from the March with an inextinguishable hope that America's promise at last would expand to embrace all races.

The Baltimore church was thriving again under Doug's leadership. His reputation for developing robust congregations was so strong that before long, he was presented with a new career opportunity in the Virgin Islands, where he was to establish two new churches. It was just the type of thing at which he excelled. With misgivings about how the move would affect the children, Mona packed up the family and they moved to the Caribbean. Although full of doubt, she prayed that it would mean a fresh start in every way.

At first, it seemed to be so. Just as Mona expected, the fledgling churches got off to a strong start. People were drawn to Doug's wise pragmatism and sought his counsel in personal as well as spiritual matters. If only he could use his own wise counsel to benefit himself, she thought.

Mona got a teaching job in the local middle school and enthusiastically entered into faculty projects and activities. With Doug busy in building up the churches, she took the role of "lead parent" at home. This included discipline when needed in the form of a switching, as she remembered her own parents administering. On one occasion when she felt the need to switch Adam, a tiny piece of twig came off and injured his eye. The closest hospital could only be reached by boat, a trip that took several hours. His hospital stay lasted over a week, and Mona was there with him throughout. It was a time for deep reflection on her love for her children, and deep regret for her actions that led to such an ordeal from Adam's minor offense.

Doug's jealousy was never far from her mind, or his. She was befriended by a neighbor named Marie, a New York transplant who joined one of Doug's new churches. They remained friends despite the fact that Marie, a lesbian, made a romantic overture which Mona quickly rebuffed. However, she later learned that Doug had enlisted Marie as a spy to report to him on Mona's comings and goings. Mona also became aware that in his office, he kept a pair of binoculars handy. The church was very near the school where she taught, and he had a clean line of sight to the entrance. Worn out by his suspicions and accusations, Mona had come to the point of not caring.

Anthony Parker taught history in the classroom next to

Mona's, and they became friends. One day out of the blue, Anthony said to her, "Mona, I believe I'm falling in love with you." Her heart pounded and every nerve in her body was alive with desire. Frustrated, unhappy and lonely, she wanted to throw herself into his arms. However, she drew strength from some unknown source to flee from the room.

That was how the affair started, and it progressed rapidly.

After so many years of being wrongly accused and struggling in vain to convince Doug of her faithfulness, Mona found it easy to respond to Anthony's ardor. They would drive high in the hills, leave the car and go to a haven that Anthony had prepared – an "earthen bed in the woods." He brought blankets and pillows from the car.

One afternoon Mona contentedly adjusted her head on the pillow and gazed into the cloudless sky. She thought to herself, *Was it John Dunne who said, 'No spring or summer beauty has such grace as I have seen in autumnal face'?*

"I love you Mona," Anthony answered. His voice brought her back to the present and she nestled closer to him. She was unable to offer a mutual declaration of love since

Doug was undeniably her love mate. But if that were the case, why was she here in another man's arms? She didn't try to condone or justify her actions. Instead she relished the delicious pleasure of being able to say, if only in her mind, *Aha Doug, finally your accusations are correct.*

Anthony's mahogany complexion glistened in the sun. Long luxurious locks rested on his shoulders. His tender caresses opened up a world of delight.

Afterward he asked, "Why are you so quiet, Mona?"

"I'm trying to figure out how our friendship grew into an affair. I never saw it coming," she replied.

"Neither did I," he responded, gently drawing her closer.

Mona shared with her lover the years of infidelity accusations that Doug had hurled at her, based on nothing but his own insecurity. She told Anthony that once before, when Priscilla was a baby, she had contemplated ending the marriage. The couple had gone through a year of counseling, and the situation improved for a time. But as with other interventions attempted for and by Doug, the change didn't last.

With Anthony she went even further in her confidences, acknowledging that Doug had not satisfied her in the bedroom. "All I ever heard growing up was Momma saying 'Don't have sex until you're married.' Doug has been my only lover. I tried for all these years to restrain my desire for an exciting sexual relationship. And now this! I doubt that our marriage will ever be firmly reestablished since I'm lying here in your arms. Why don't I feel any guilt?"

Mona waited for a response. "Tony, are you asleep? I don't think you've heard a word I said!"

"I did not miss a word, my darling," he replied. "I marvel at the similarity of our experiences."

Now it was Anthony's turn to confide. He had grown up in Chicago, in a housing project of poorly constructed row houses that required the residents to bring in pot-bellied stoves and electric heaters to stay warm. He had been 10 years old when his father left. His mother struggled to make ends meet as a domestic worker, leaving Anthony in charge of his six year old brother and instructing them to let no one in the house and not to go outside under any circumstances. He had lived within his own fence, of a sort.

Anthony's mother had also warned him to avoid trouble in school, steer clear of drugs and not fool around with the girls, because they'd get him in trouble. He excelled in school and won scholarships for college. Seeing the impact of alcohol and drugs on some of his classmates, he left them alone. But when it came to girls ....

He had been forced to marry at age 18 after getting his girlfriend pregnant. She had miscarried, and after several months they agreed to part. For several years Anthony had been involved in numerous affairs, gaining a reputation as a "player." Then at 25 he had given marriage another chance, but his new wife Claudia couldn't abide the thought that he might return to his former philandering ways. This fear had driven her away.

Similar indeed!

Mona knew that Doug was suspicious of her friendship with Anthony but didn't care. One night as he harangued her, she repeated the insult she had uttered that night in Dover – "you can't satisfy me." For a second time, he reacted with physical violence against her. As Mona fled from the room, she passed her youngest daughter and realized that Priscilla had witnessed everything.

Mona and Doug realized they had reached the breaking

point of their marriage. Doug told her to take the children to Chester and leave them with her mother, then come back so they could work on rebuilding their relationship without parenting distractions. Mona agreed to do so, knowing all along she would not return.

In Chester, Mona once again enrolled the children in local schools. She found a job and informed Doug of her intention to stay put. Anthony had followed her and enrolled in grad school nearby. They picked up their relationship where they had left off in the Virgin Islands, in spite of the fact that Mona was seeing a counselor who sternly advised her against continuing the affair while married.

No one in her family knew what was going on. They had no notion of Anthony or of the possibility of an irreparable breach between Mona and Doug. He sent her and the children a monthly allowance, which suggested that all was well. Her mother and sisters accepted her explanation about the separation – "It was no place for a family, no place for the kids." The assumption was that Doug would finish his Virgin Islands assignment and rejoin her and the children. Mona did nothing to suggest otherwise – not openly anyway. She frequently met Anthony at a hotel, paying little heed to the counselor's advice and amazed at how quiet her own conscience remained.

# Chapter Thirteen

## CONNECTIONS, BROKEN AND REVIVED

**AFTER PARTING WITH DOUG** at the airport, Mona and the children left for Chester. She had the first opportunity since her marriage to spend extensive time with her family. She and the children lived in the Reaney Street home. The emotional distance between Madeline and Josiah was as great as ever, maybe more so. While her parents' relationship was discouraging, especially in light of her own estrangement, Mona found pleasure in reuniting with her sisters. Just like her, she learned that much had changed in their lives.

Laura and Dimetra had become close, drawn together by a common interest in gardening and travel. It blossomed suddenly. Sipping lemonade in Dimetra's backyard one day, Laura had admired the symmetry of an elm on the lot. "What a magnificent tree!" she remarked. "The leaves seem to dance in the breeze."

"I agree," said Dimetra. "I love sitting out here in the early mornings. Even as the day heats up, the sun never seems to penetrate its coolness."

When Laura noted that her own elm, planted at the same time as Dimetra's, was not doing as well, her sister offered to root a cutting for Laura to plant. That conversation seemed to open a new chapter in their relationship. Both divorced, they began taking trips together and sharing gardening secrets. Laura had developed a fascination with Dimetra's collection of antiques and curios, the product of many flea market visits.

By this time Dimetra had achieved a life of comfortable independence, which Mona admired. Her six years of marriage to indolent Don had ended soon after the birth of their only child, a daughter named Gail. The couple divorced, and Don quickly faded from their lives.

Building on her success with Kessler Beauty Products, Dimetra also had started a hairdressing business. Increasingly confident in her ability to make her own way, she and young Gail moved to a three-bedroom cottage just outside Jersey City. On her one-acre lot, she put her gardening skills to work to supplement her income from beauty products and hair styling, setting up a sidewalk stand with vegetables, fruit and herbs.

Over time, a third business emerged for Dimetra, selling antiques and collectibles. With Gail in tow, she visited galleries and antique shops, her daughter's auburn braids dancing in the wind as she trailed alongside her mother. One day Gail urged Dimetra to bid on an 18th century Canterbury pitcher and bowl, and a new enterprise was born. Soon she was regularly selling and trading antiques with friends and neighbors as eager customers.

Dimetra eventually remarried. She met Ronald one Saturday morning at a local antique shop. His six-foot frame towered over small Dimetra. Along with antiques they shared an interest in gardening and entertaining. Indeed, it was a coveted privilege to be invited to their backyard parties featuring barbecued ribs, fried fish, collard greens and okra, fresh from their garden – and to enjoy the delicious meal surrounded by their beautiful roses and fragrant flowers of various ravishing colors.

However, even as Mona observed her sister's industry and accomplishments with admiration, she couldn't help but wonder why Dimetra paid so little attention to the care of her home, in contrast to the beautiful and carefully tended gardens. Although bought as inventory to re-sell, Dimetra had a hard time parting with many of her purchases. Dusty "treasures" piled up on shelves, neglected in favor of her true passions of gardening, fishing and cooking. Mona personally found the condition of Dimetra's home deplorable, but also noted that guests seemed to ignore it. Just as in their younger years, people either avoided Dimetra altogether, or embraced her prickly and eccentric ways.

For a time, Mona also enjoyed a warm reunion with her sister Erica who lived nearby. Erica, the family dreamer, had always exerted a special hold on her siblings. Following the hurt and disappointment of her first marriage, Erica had accomplished her goal of marrying into affluent society. Her second husband, Sean, was wealthy and well connected. They moved in a circle of professionals with ample means to entertain and to travel, which Erica enjoyed immensely.

She and Sean invited interesting guests to elegant parties in their home. Sean was a perfect host, and Erica was eager to bring Mona into their social scene. While Mona's suitcase stayed at her parents, she spent most of her days at Erica's home.

Then abruptly, Erica rescinded the open invitation. "Mona, I've decided that you and I should spend less time together," she said one day. "Sean and I have been entertaining too often, and I feel that it's putting too much stress on our relationship. Just last night after the guests left, we had an hour-long shouting match."

Mona was taken aback. "I promise to keep clear of the two of you," she replied. "Why can't I come over anymore?"

"Not for a while," Erica insisted. We need time to resolve some of our issues." Mona pressed for more insight. "Erica, what did I do? Do I share any blame in this trouble between the two of you? Are you jealous of me?"

Instantly Mona realized her words were a mistake, implying that Sean might have taken a fancy to her.

Erica snapped back, "Why should I be jealous of you? I'm quite capable of taking care of Sean's needs!" She stormed off in a fit of rage.

Stunned, Mona began to reflect on moments that Erica might have misread as a Sean-Mona flirtation. She instantly thought of the party that previous evening when Sean had pulled her aside and shown her a mass of money he had taken from a pouch. Mona's reaction had been instinctive and loud. "My God, look at all that money." Everyone in the room had turned their attention toward Sean's stack of bills.

Mona had wondered at Erica's reaction – "He never shows me his money." While she had not thought much about it at the time, now the situation took on a different significance.

Other occasions came to mind. She had once mentioned to Erica that her allowance from Doug had not arrived as normal. Evidently Sean was listening because he called her upstairs just a moment later with an offer to lend her money. She had refused it with assurance that she was certain the check would arrive soon. Later she mentioned his offer casually to Erica. It had not seemed to Mona as anything but a generous gesture from a family member. Maybe Erica saw it differently.

Her thoughts even went back many years to the episode with their cousin Reuben. Each sister had been unaware of the other's involvement with Reuben, or that he was filling both their heads with hopeless daydreams. When the situation came to light, their mother had immediately taken Erica's side and attacked Mona for "sneaking around" with Erica's boyfriend. That's how Erica must have seen the matter as well. The hurtful memories from those long-ago days welled up to match her present hurt at Erica's rejection. Mona regretted that she had never cleared things up about Reuben and brought closure around it with her sister.

Now it seemed too late. Erica had no intention of softening toward her younger sister, which brought untold sorrow to Mona's heart and the deepest sense of loss and grief she had ever felt. She wrote a tear-drenched letter to Erica asking forgiveness for any pain she had caused. Several days later the letter was returned marked "wrong address."

The estrangement from Erica compounded a growing sadness about Doug. Although she had not broken off with Anthony, she missed her husband. Around this time, she and the children moved to Philadelphia, because she had been hired to teach in an early childhood development program called Get Set, in the county school district. It was a good job that paid well, but she didn't know anyone there.

For the next year Mona traveled a lonely road. A childhood friend who practiced divorce law had convinced Mona to start divorce preparations, although Mona had misgivings. She felt that in every direction she looked, her family life was unraveling. Madeline's health was declining, and Josiah's bitterness at life in general seemed ever stronger.

Increasingly sensitive to the importance of blood relations, Mona made another effort to reach Erica by letter. She wrote with great caution, assuming all blame for the rupture between them and asking for forgiveness. Erica's response drove the dagger of pain deeper in Mona's heart – a two-sentence reply that read, "I'd rather not hear from you anymore. Please just leave me alone."

Mona pressed her other sisters for any explanation they possibly could give her about Erica's anger. Stella, Laura and Dimetra were now included in Erica's lavish parties and social activities. Erica always had a way of inducing a hypnotic state over her siblings, making them accept any suggestion she made. What had she told them? To Mona's questions, the older sisters gave only vague answers that illuminated nothing and left her frustrated and forlorn.

# *Chapter Fourteen*

## A FRESH BEGINNING

**MEANWHILE DOUG WAS CALLING** constantly. Pleas for reconciliation accompanied his monthly checks. Mona felt herself softening toward him as she read his plaintiff declarations of love, recalling happier times when their union seemed perfect. He also conveyed his respect for her ability to make a new life on her own. She realized that her independent success had given him much to think about.

"Mona, I know you have been enjoying your freedom away from me," he wrote. "You're the kind of person who can adapt to any situation. Please give me another chance. I promise to never hit you again."

Lonely and unsatisfied without him, she relented and agreed to his return on two conditions – no more accusations or physical abuse, and they would go to counseling as a couple. The affair with Anthony already had faded. She knew she still loved Doug, and she also wanted her family to be complete. The children were growing up. They needed their father and a united home. Also in the depth of her thoughts, she wanted to spare her mother the distress of another of her children going through divorce. Doug agreed to the conditions. Mona felt he would have agreed to anything to be allowed back into her life.

This belief soon was confirmed. Unpacking his books, she found a journal in his handwriting. It surprised her, as she had never known him to keep a diary in the past. She realized these writings covered the period of her absence and could tell from several entries that the psychiatrist he was seeing encouraged him to write. Without hesitation she read every word.

Doug's writings were tortured with guilt, sadness and fear that each new ring of the phone would be a call from Mona that she was divorcing him. He wrote that few parishioners seem convinced that she had left for the sake of the children's schooling. Speculation was rampant, which added to his burdens. Yet it also seemed to relieve him that the truth of their situation was generally understood. He wrote that he had informed the bishop of their separation.

Occasionally he mentioned being invited to a social event. On his birthday several friends had entertained him at the beach. While he had enjoyed the day, the underlying sadness welled up from the pages. No cards had come from the children. Mona's conscience pricked her that she hadn't prompted them to remember their father's birthday.

In his writings Doug frankly acknowledged his responsibility for damaging, perhaps even destroying their marriage. He freely described a constant wrestling match with the demon of jealousy, and expressed desperate fear that the demon had cost him what he cherished most in the world.

Mona was stunned at the intensity and honesty of the passages. She had never realized the depth of Doug's suffering, the torment that wracked him both for the fear of losing her and the shame of knowing he had driven her away because he was enslaved by possessiveness and distrust.

Along with surprise, Mona read the diary with some guilt.

Over time, she had built up deep anger because of his jealous rages, draining any empathy she might otherwise feel for his struggles. Reading the journal tapped into a deeper well of compassion. With this new insight into his state of mind, Mona felt cautiously optimistic that going to couples counseling might help them find healing with each other.

Over the next year, they participated in a group with four other couples. Doug showed no reluctance to go, and a revived spirit of cooperation emerged between him and Mona. In the group conversations, Mona began to consider that their problems might not have been as one-sided as she always had assumed. Doug had long accused her of being a flirt. As this was discussed in the group, one of the other men turned and said to her, "Well, you ARE a flirt." She was startled and shaken to the point of fleeing the room for a time.

Doug's earnest efforts to restore their relationship caused her to reflect on positive qualities of his that she had not thought about in a while. She had always credited him with being a good father, encouraging the children's generosity and kind-heartedness. Now she realized, as never before, his beneficial influence on herself as well.

"Mona is a spoiled brat," Madeline had told Doug before

they married. "You'll need to take a firm hand." Yes, she had been spoiled. Mona acknowledged now that he had helped to change her pouty ways. When she was upset and prone to sulk, he refused to let her brood in silence, drawing her out to express her feelings.

Now, to his credit, he accepted a reversal of their roles with good grace. She was the main bread winner while Doug searched for a suitable church appointment. The diocese appointed him to lead a small congregation in Philadelphia and do development work with other congregations in the area. Doug also began work on a doctorate in sociology at Temple University and took an assistant instructor position at La Salle University.

His new emotional stability came with a price, however. The old jealousy was gone, but there was not much spark in its place. Doug had never enjoyed social life and seemed less inclined that way than ever. Mona found him dull. He worked hard, and when home, he would sit in front of the TV until he nodded off for the evening. When they would entertain guests, he would often disappear, and she would find him upstairs watching a football game. "Doug, why have you left our guests?" she would ask in irritation. Grudgingly he would return.

While this behavior embarrassed Mona, she couldn't help

but notice that their guests didn't seem to interpret it as rudeness. Whether he disappeared entirely or simply withdrew from conversation, they seemed to regard his uncommunicative ways as a sign of deep thought. As had always been true, Doug was regarded with the highest respect among parishioners, fellow clergy and their circle of friends.

For Mona, marriage was now comfortable and safe, but uninspiring. She could feel herself getting restless. A female friend in the neighborhood persuaded her to visit a club in the area. The friend's husband was a policeman, and somehow that made Mona feel easier about the club visits. Yet her memories of the Anthony episode were fresh enough that she started to sense danger, so much so that she pushed Doug to relocate the family to another neighborhood.

The family moved but stayed connected to the former church, where Mona and daughter Priscilla had started an after-school program for neighborhood youth. Four afternoons a week, kids would come to the program for homework help and activities that kept them out of trouble. This meant long days for Mona, but she was truly devoted to working with the community children. Decades later, she remained in touch with several of the now-grown children whose appreciation and love for her endured into their own adult years.

The Cartwright children had reached an age and maturity that intersected with the growing momentum of the Civil Rights Movement. Since that day when Mona and Doug had marched in Washington, the shift in national mood had become profound. Congress had passed laws that began to deliver on long-withheld promises. Increasingly, people of color were emboldened to take to the streets to advance those promises – especially students. Threats, bombings and Ku Klux Klan marches did little to deter them. They increasingly embraced their African heritage in their choice of hairstyles, dress and cultural practices. Miriam, Adam and Priscilla participated in the zeitgeist.

Doug and Mona had raised their offspring to be compassionate and action-oriented, attributes which were well suited to the times. Adam founded an organization called AFNET and worked as a community organizer to empower Philadelphia's poor with the will, capabilities and resources to chart a more assertive and ambitious course for themselves. There were risks as well as opportunities in such actions, as AFNET drew regular scrutiny from the police. It was rumored in the neighborhood that Doug's church phone was being monitored.

Even so, the family felt the exhilaration of involvement in the historic change that was sweeping the country. The opportunity to advance this spirit often came in one-to-one encounters in the community. If a youth needed a place to stay, Priscilla's solution was to bring him or her to the parish house for a few nights – or longer. A young girl whose mother had died recently became a regular visitor.

One night Mona and Doug arrived home from a dinner to find a homeless family of four bedded down in the living room. Priscilla had encountered them and brought them to the parish house. Doug found a shelter to take them in.

The family also hosted various cousins who were having trouble at home. Rare was the time when an extra soul or two wasn't on hand in the Cartwright household. The social transformation abroad in the country converged with their own impulse to lighten someone else's load. Somehow there was always enough resource, energy and patience to reach out to others who needed a lift.

# Chapter Fifteen

## ENCOUNTER

**SURVIVORS OF TRAUMATIC INJURY** often do not recall the physical impact or the immediate events leading up to it. Mona remembered every detail.

It was wintertime, with a windy chill in the air. As was her mid-week custom, the organist at Doug's church had practiced late into the evening. Doug and Mona always drove her home. This night, another church member was with them. The organist had invited them all for dinner, serving a spicy dish from her native Jamaica. She also offered her guests strong Jamaican rum.

The rum had its effect, and the Cartwrights and fellow church member all left the organist's home in a drowsy state. Mona sat in the middle of the front seat to make room for their extra passenger. Within a few blocks, she had dozed off. Unfortunately, so had Doug and their passenger. The blue Chevrolet jumped the curb and slammed into a small store that sat flush against the corner. Mona took the brunt of the impact. She jolted to her left and landed hard against the steering wheel. Although semi-conscious, the sight of Doug's eyeglasses shattered on the car floor registered clearly in her mind. So did the stabbing pain she felt inside. Miraculously the others in the car were not hurt.

Rushed to the emergency room, Mona was given a cursory examination and x-ray. The nurse told Doug there was no evidence of broken bones, to take her home and put her on bed rest for several days.

At home, Mona lay in excruciating pain, barely able to move. Doug walked in and out of her room, smoking cigarettes, as if in a trance. Priscilla was alarmed by her mother's groans and refused to be reassured by Doug's recounting of the nurse's instructions. She called Miriam, now a college freshman, who hurried home. They managed to get Mona to Dr. Steinbeck, her gynecologist, who immediately recognized multiple serious injuries: broken shoulder blade; broken ribs; and a ruptured spleen which was bleeding and required immediate surgery.

Following the operation, Mona was placed in a ward with six other patients due to a shortage of private rooms. She began to feel better quickly. Needing to visit the bathroom, she was helped by a nurse in managing the IV roller as they moved along. Walking through the ward, Mona delighted her fellow patients by shaking her hips. "You just had surgery, and you're dancing!" they shouted almost in unison.

Alone in the bathroom, Mona looked out the window into a tangle of pipes, vents and conduits above the building next door. "Not much of a view," she thought. As she prepared to return to her bed, suddenly she was aware of a calm, serene spirit coming over her. It drew her away from the window to the middle of the room. She felt overwhelmed by awesome fear. "Lord, what are you trying to tell me? Why am I feeling this way?" she wondered. She hastened to exit the room, practically dragging the IV rod behind her.

Back in her hospital bed, Mona's thoughts raced. She had no doubt that God was commanding her attention. She had never felt like this before, despite growing up in a church-going family. This was a power of a different sort. "Lord, what are you trying to tell me?" Mona cried out aloud, again and again. She couldn't stop weeping.

Back at home, the conversion experience continued. She was visited by several friends including a woman named Leona, in whose home Mona had once attended a weekly Bible study. Mona remembered the intimacy Leona seemed to have had with God as she prayed, how easily she spoke to her "precious Jesus."

Now Leona interpreted what was happening to Mona, and the effect was like an anointing. "Honey, that's the presence of the Holy Spirit that is healing you – body, mind and spirit," Leona said.

Another of the friends, Mildred, spoke up. "I felt that God was sending us here for a reason. I almost said 'no' when Leona invited me to join her."

Mona replied tearfully, "It's as if a heavy burden is falling from my shoulders."
In her weakened and injured state, God had reached her, and taken hold of her as never before.

As a 12-year old, Mona had stood up in the Baptist church and professed faith in Christ mainly to escape the mourner's bench, the front-row pew reserved for the not-yet-converted. Even so, she had believed there was a Godly presence in the world for as long as she could remember. And while as a priest's wife in the staid

Episcopal Church, she was thankful that no mourner's bench intruded, the fervor of the religion she had observed as a child stayed with her and remain a strong influence. However, this new fervor was of an entirely different order from her previous religious experiences, Baptist or Episcopal. It consumed her, never leaving her mind, relentlessly shaping her thoughts and actions. She felt a constant restless yearning to be with people who professed and worshipped Jesus. This yearning was not to be resisted.

A co-worker, Mrs. McKeither, came to mind. Mrs. McKeither attended an evangelical church and shared her faith freely among her work colleagues. On more than one occasion, she had told her, "Mona, the Lord wants you." At the time Mona had shrugged it off with a flippant reply, "He'll have to wait until I've had some fun. I've been cooped up all my life."

Now it seemed that the Lord had waited long enough. Mona sought out Mrs. McKeither's church for worship and prayer services. She began visiting other spirited churches as well, drawn by the fervor. Still recovering from her injuries and supposed to be on bed rest, she had to sneak out of the house to pursue deeper knowledge. As soon as Doug was out of sight on his way to the university, she headed to one of the local evangelical churches that her parents had called "holy roller." She became friends with several of the worshipers, who would pray and lay hands on her. Mona couldn't get enough of these experiences, feeling an unquenchable thirst to hear the Word of God preached along with powerful prayer. "It was like a honeymoon between God and me," Mona later said of this time.

She became deeply involved in Bible study, where the scripture came alive in a way she had never grasped before. As the New Testament commanded, she "prayed without ceasing" for a guide to appear who could lead her deeper into faith and scriptural insight. "I know I need help," she told one of her new friends.

At one of the evangelical churches she frequented, such a guide appeared. She was a former missionary named Florence Tilly. Nearly 70, Florence had grown up in England, left for the mission field as a young adult, spending decades in Kenya. Now she had retired in the US to be near her sisters.

Florence had exhaustive Biblical knowledge which she freely shared. She became one of Mona's closest friends as well as a strong influence on her spiritual growth, bringing her into a second group for Bible study. Just as chapter 7 of Revelation promised, Mona felt that she was being guided to the "springs of the water of life." Bible study became one of her principal joys. She absorbed it like a sponge, wrestling with challenging passages and tracing the powerful and often surprising ways in which God worked to pour out His love and effect His will.

As highly as Mona regarded Florence's expertise on the Bible, their applications of scripture didn't always agree. One point of difference concerned asking for God's blessings. Florence contended that when people, especially poor people, didn't get what they asked for, it was because they didn't know how to ask. Mona doubted this. "I've known mostly poor people all my life," she countered, "and they knew how to ask." Mona believed that the full measure of grace was to find the blessing in what God gave, whether it had been asked for or not.

Another difference between Mona and Florence was evident in how they taught youth, which they began to do together on Bible study retreats in the Pocono Mountains. Once there had been a profession of faith, Florence tended to go quickly to the "do's and don'ts" implications. Mona's approach was to emphasize the richness of relationship with the Savior, avoiding the notion that faith was about rules and regulations.

Attending adult retreats organized by prominent

evangelists and preachers became one of Mona's most ardent endeavors. The Poconos were a favorite spot for these events. She met people from all kinds of churches, mostly women, who had all manner of stories to tell. One night one of the women in Mona's cabin told of being rescued from a violent storm, and Mona listened quietly, tears streaming down her face.

Most of the people she met on the retreats were good company, but a few were less so. On one retreat a small group urged her to join them in an experience of glossolalia, or speaking in tongues. Mona did sit in with them but felt nothing happening, which seemed to raise questions in their minds about the authenticity of her faith. When she went off to pray alone, a few women followed her and insisted on praying and laying on hands. One of the women began screaming in a Satanic sort of way. Mona wondered how could you speak in tongues one minute, and be in such deep pain the next?

Meanwhile, Doug struggled to accept the change that had taken place in Mona. He felt that she was rejecting his way of worship and expressed skepticism about much of the joy and learning she described after the retreats. At last she convinced him to come with her (actually she felt that the Lord convinced him.)

At the retreat site where they went together, there was a place in a nearby field designated for anyone who needed to go for a smoke. It was marked with a sign that read "Egypt." If you had to go down to Egypt, it meant you had not yet been delivered from the compulsion to smoke. You were still enslaved. Doug, a longtime heavy smoker, was determined not to go down to Egypt – so much so that he quit and never smoked again.

Throughout this time of her "honeymoon with God," Mona never asked for proof of His power, but she received verification more than once. One night she prayed for Madeline's recovery from a long and painful bout with shingles. At one of the holiness churches she was attending, she told her fellow worshipers about her mother's illness. They prayed fervently as one that Madeline would experience healing. Mona found out from her mother that she had begun to make a stunning improvement the very next day. It was the first of what would be many prayer-related healings Mona would witness in the years to come.

Meanwhile, her sisters doubted that Mona's change was permanent. "Oh you'll move on to something else before long," Stella said, and Laura and Dimetra concurred. Madeline, on the other hand, had no doubt that God had now engaged Mona in a singular and lasting way. She was delighted at this development, with one exception. She rebuked Mona for doubting the sincerity of her salvation at age 12. Mourner's bench or not, Madeline was convinced that Mona's profession had been authentic. This new experience was just a deeper level of what her daughter already had, Madeline was quite sure.

# Chapter Sixteen

## BORN AGAIN

**IN THE AFTERMATH OF** her theophany and immersion in God's presence, Mona lived the reality of a transformation described by evangelist and writer Oswald Chambers, *"... having received a continual surprise of the life of God: a perennial, eternal and perpetual (PEP) beginning, a freshness all the time in thinking and in talking and in living."*

Skeptics typically discount intense religious experiences like Mona's as arising from psychological stress. In her specific case they might point to a weakened body following the accident and surgery, or the emotional trauma of a close brush with death, or even unresolved marital matters. Although Mona had many questions, she never doubted the authenticity of what had happened, or that its source was external to her own mind. She had been touched, spoken to, and altered from an outward power that bore no resemblance to anything emotional or psychological. The doubts of skeptics troubled her not at all, rather they confirmed the warnings of scripture to be prepared for disbelief, misunderstanding and even open hostility.

In her new spiritual estate, Mona believed the promise of God completely as fulfilled in Christ. *"Therefore if anyone is in Christ, s/he is a new creation. Old things are passed away. Behold, all things are become new."* (2nd Corinthians 5:17) This constant sense of "newness" was one of the exhilarating aspects of her change.

She turned a small room in the house into a "secret place" for communion with God, starting with morning prayer. *"In the morning, O Lord, Thou wilt hear my voice."* (Psalm 5:3) Again, before lying down at night, she recounted the Lord's promise to *"command His lovingkindness in the daytime and his song to be with her in the night."* (Psalm 42:8). Memorizing scriptures became natural to her.
The words that Jesus had said to Nicodemus were constantly in her mind: *"The wind blows wherever it pleases. You hear its sound but you cannot tell where it comes from or where it is going. So it is with everyone*

*born of the Spirit."* (John 3:8). She had first felt the wind of the Spirit in the strangest of places – a hospital restroom, stitched back together after surgery, poked by tubes and hanging onto an IV pole. But felt it she had, as surely as if she had been in the crowd at Pentecost or traveling with Paul to Damascus.

In the weeks and months that followed, she experienced immensely fulfilling dimensions of existence; deep prayer, Bible study, fellowship and service. In time she came to know that no matter what pain or sorrow might touch her life from here on, it could never suppress the joy and hope of owning the love of Jesus Christ in the depths of her being.

At the elementary school where she now was teaching, Mona began leading a teachers' Bible study before classes started. It was well attended, including two Jewish participants. In spite of prohibitions against Christian teachings in public school classrooms, Mona didn't hesitate to share her faith with students as well. The neighborhood was heavily Italian and Catholic, so the mention of Jesus didn't ruffle feathers. She did receive one complaint from a non-believing parent whose son was upset when Mona enlisted prayer for a classmate whose grandfather had died. Other than making sure she avoided topics of faith around that particular student,

Mona continued to express her faith. Some of the children, and their families, were deeply influenced. One set of parents even came to Cape May for a retreat.

Mona had newfound courage to share her faith with others, yet the movement of the Spirit could be frightening, pushing her beyond comfort. "When the Spirit first comes to you," she later said, "there is fear and doubt. My thought was, 'This is not me, this is not what I want to do.'"

She was asked to speak to a Philadelphia women's group. It came to her mind that she should confess her infidelity, but she put the thought away. Yet while speaking, Mona felt led to share this part of her life. Some in the audience wept. Others seemed confused. There had been a time when this confession would have been impossible for her. But she knew she had been set free and believed "when the Lord has set you free, you are free indeed."

She came to understand that her personal desires could no longer rule her life. Her very essence was now at God's disposal, even when His guidance led her into uncomfortable circumstances.

All her life Mona had a way of drawing people to her and holding the attraction. This natural vivaciousness had contributed to the breach with Erica and at times had caused her aggravation when admirers became "clingy." If a new friendship heated too quickly, Mona's longtime inclination was to become cool and to distance herself.

But now God turned the tables on her, using the magnetic qualities of her personality for His purposes. Whether she liked it or not, people were pulled to her as a fount of spirituality, wisdom and guidance. The little prayer room she had established as a "secret place" for divine communion became busy with a steady flow of seekers, old and young. They sensed that she carried the spark of the Lord, and they came close in the hopes of feeling its warmth and possibly gaining clarity from its light.

They unloaded their burdens in front of her. "I'm living a wicked life. I'm having an affair with a married man." This confession came from a much younger woman whom Mona had met in Bible study. Her first impression of the young woman had been negative – Mona thought she had a flippant attitude and seemed unserious about it all. Gradually the flippancy disappeared as awareness dawned on the woman of the distance between where she was in relation to God, and where she felt she needed to be. Sensing Mona's closeness to the Lord, she began coming to the prayer room.

Another woman asked to come, and as soon as she arrived she announced, "I'm going to divorce my husband. He didn't tell me he had a 12 year old daughter until right before we married."

A young woman came to Mona after her husband left her. She had sacrificed her own career to put him through graduate school and now was deeply disillusioned. "I've tried every known religion. None satisfies me. What should I do?"

Still another brought the bitter fruit of a long-ago choice. "I gave up my son for adoption years ago. Now my heart yearns for him."

With each visitor, Mona prayed, asking the Lord to take the situation and make of it what He would. Occasionally she felt led to give counsel. To the woman angry at her husband for not disclosing his adolescent child, Mona gave her a paper and pen, told her to divide the paper in half and list his strengths and weaknesses. It was a clarifying moment, illuminating for the woman that the blessings of her marriage far outweighed the grievance she was nursing.

Mona had become an insatiable reader of spiritual reflections, especially mystics like Thomas R. Kelly, a

Quaker. In his *Testament of Devotion*, Kelly came close to describing what Mona had experienced.

*"There comes a time when the Presence steals upon us. Out of the plain of daily living suddenly looms such plateaus. Before we know it we are walking upon their heights and all the old familiar landscape becomes new. One walks in the world, yet above the world, giddy with the height; peace, utter peace and security! The past matters less and the future even less, for the NOW contains all that is needed for the absolute satisfaction of our deepest cravings; the holy NOW; 'a joy unspeakable and full of glory'"*

Some of those whom Mona counseled had ears open to understand such thoughts. Others were not yet ready, yet a steady diet of writers like Kelly and Thomas Merton fortified her to attend patiently to their needs, trusting that they gradually would become ready to move from spiritual milk to solid meat, per St. Paul's description in I Corinthians 3:2.

As more people, especially women, sought her for spiritual counseling, dealing with the pain and confusion of others took a toll on Mona's own store of emotional energy. Yet she always found replenishment, as promised in the Book of Lamentations. *"It is of the LORD's mercies that*

*we are not consumed, because his compassions fail not.*
*They are new every morning: great is thy faithfulness."*
*(Lamentations 3:22-23)*

Two episodes provided especially vivid confirmation of
the Lord's faithfulness as she found courage to work with
others in His name.

Doug had never overcome his boyhood resentment of his
mother's coldness and lack of attention to him. Mona
could see that Elizabeth's failure to be a nurturing parent
stemmed from being an unwed mother at a time when
society was unforgiving about such things. But Mona
also could see that this was no consolation to Doug,
who had experienced so much pain from his mother's
emotional neglect.

In her elderly years, she had developed severe diabetes
but did not take good care of herself. She wound up in
a nursing home and developed bedsores. Convinced of
God's will in the matter, Mona insisted that they bring
her to their home. Doing so would mean great sacrifice
including paying for in-home care for Elizabeth. After
initial resistance, Doug agreed with Mona that they
should take this huge step. He made arrangements. Two
days before the move was to happen, his mother passed
away.

At her funeral, Doug gave the eulogy. Mona could see that he had truly forgiven his mother at last. His forgiving spirit made her death a time of healing.

The other episode was more dramatic still. A wealthy doctor in Doug's old Baltimore parish had died and left Doug in charge of a trust that paid the man's adult son an allowance. The son was wild and extravagant, always wanting Doug to increase or advance the money he was due.

The son, whose name was George, still lived in Baltimore and had started a small business making leather vests. His money demands intensified. One night when Doug was away at a meeting, George showed up at their home, making threats if he didn't get more money. He already had threatened harm on the phone. Now he banged on the front door; Mona and Priscilla prayed inside. Then Mona went to the door and invited him to sit down with her on the porch.

What a sight to behold! George, in his early 30s, was nearly 6 feet tall. He stared at Mona from greenish grey eyes. His clean shaven "cocoa" complexion contrasted sharply with the dark curly braids that hung on his shoulders. A short open leather vest failed to cover his hairy body. A wide leather belt was struggling to keep his tight pants from revealing even more of his hairy body. Leather boots rose to cover his knees. George looked as fearsome as his threats.

Mona prayed silently: *"Holy Spirit, I need you! You tell me what to say to this young man."*

She turned to him, "George, do you believe in Jesus?"

George retorted, "No! I have traveled all over the Middle East and studied most of the religions of the great prophets, including Jesus. His story, to me, is the craziest of all. If He had been as powerful as he had claimed to be, why did He allow himself to become a spectacle on the cross?"

Mona replied, "George, He did it for you."

"I don't think so," George shot back. "Why would I need a person to save me who couldn't even save Himself?"

"George," said Mona, "I need you to do me a favor. Would you allow me to introduce you to Jesus as I know Him?" With a look of doubt on his face, George assented.

Mona got her Bible and started reading the salvation

story to George. He began to ask questions. She read St. Paul's words that "all have sinned and fallen short." (Romans 3:23). As the night wore on, she began to pray with George. He stayed until 1 a.m., by which time he had made a confession of sin and invited Jesus into his life. He asked Mona for a Bible. He left in a state of excitement and told her later that he had read the Bible on the train all the way back to Baltimore.

Shortly afterwards, George was back in touch. "You forgot to teach me how to pray," he said. Then he told her of men coming to his shop late one night, banging on the door (as he had done at Mona's home.) He knew it was his creditors coming for payment he could not make. Desperate, he kneeled down and prayed a simple word – "Help." Letting them in, he was stunned to realize that instead of the creditors he had feared, they were men who owed him money for goods and had come to pay him. Help indeed.

Through Doug's forgiveness of his mother, George's amazing deliverance, and countless other events, Mona found herself living, day after day, Oswald Chambers' "continual surprise of the life of God."

# Chapter Seventeen

## TURNING TIDES

**IF ANYONE HAD SUGGESTED** to Mona that the spiritual abundance she felt would yield material prosperity, she would have dismissed the thought out of hand. It was sheer coincidence her new life in Christ fell at a time of improving economic circumstances for the family.

She convinced Doug to buy a summer beach home at Cape May, New Jersey, just a two-hour drive from Philadelphia. Both of them yearned for a place to get away and enjoy quiet and privacy. They both loved the shore, and for Mona it was part of her early memories. Madeline had worked as a domestic for a wealthy family who spent a week each summer at the Atlantic City seashore. She would accompany the family, bringing Mona who was barely more than a toddler. Mona remembered playing in the sand and letting the waves wash over her. Now she wanted to come and go to the beach whenever she chose – and to bring Madeline as a guest rather than a maid.

Cape May was a favorite resort for African Americans, and many owned homes there. She and Doug investigated and visited various properties up for sale. It didn't take long for her to see the beach house of her dreams. She told Doug to stop in front of the house and proceeded to do something she had never done before in her life – to ask God for a specific intervention to gain a material beneficence. She prayed that they would get this particular house.

Inside, meeting the real estate agent, she dispensed with niceties. "I want this house and I want you to sell it to us for $12,000," she said. Even in the 1960s, that would be quite a bargain for Cape May property. The agent's mouth fell open and he said nothing for several seconds. Then he smiled and said, "Little lady, I'll tell you what. I'll take $12,000, just for you."

The house at Cape May became a place of retreat for the family, and even more a place of fellowship with relatives and friends. Every summer Mona brought her sisters to the shore for a reunion. Stella and Laura loved the comings and goings of Cartwright friends. Dimetra preferred family-only gatherings, and Erica kept her distance altogether.

Along with her prayer room in Philadelphia, Cape May became a hub for Mona's spiritual retreats and counseling sessions. Groups of women, including fellow wives of clergy, would join her at the shore for study and prayer. When counseling was in order, she would hold individual conversations in a small tent, which originally had been set up in the yard for her grandchildren's amusement. Mona could not help but smile at the Lord's creativity, using a child's hideaway as a place for holy dialogue and help.

Ever the teacher and mentor, Mona turned Cape May into "Camp May" for four incorrigible young boys from her elementary school. She wanted them to have an experience dramatically different from inner city Philadelphia. Putting them to work in her garden, she delighted that these boys who were uncontrollable at school took to their cultivation assignments with eagerness and discipline. Even when she learned with dismay that the Cartwright children's piggy banks had been pilfered, Mona felt it worth the investment to show them a side of life dramatically different than what they were accustomed to.

When Madeline came to Cape May, it was a special joy. Mona reveled that her mother now could visit the seashore as an honored guest, not an overworked domestic. By now Josiah and Madeline had left Reaney Street, their property having been purchased for $6300 by the state for highway right of way. Even though the house was in bad condition, Mona's parents grieved at the loss. Not only did Reaney Street hold precious memories, they had to give up the comfortable income the store had provided, along with the pleasure of being positively involved with their neighbors on an almost daily basis.

Their children saw the situation differently. Madeline and Josiah were well past retirement age and not in good health. The daughters found a one-bedroom apartment for them in a pleasant, federally subsidized complex. Located at the corner of a building, the sunlit apartment offered garden space for Madeline to grow roses and clematis. There were fishing lakes nearby, so she and Josiah could continue their favorite pastime – the only time together that seemed to bring them into genuine peace and harmony.

Madeline and Josiah had lived in the apartment for a

year when Josiah died suddenly. He had been standing at the dresser, arranging his necktie for church, when he collapsed of a stroke. Mona and Doug got the news within an hour but were delayed in coming to Chester because one of Doug's parishioners was also close to death. Doug pastored her family through the final hours, then he, Mona and the children drove through the dark to Madeline's little apartment.

There, they found Madeline surrounded by sympathetic love and support from friends and neighbors. Over the next few days, the outpouring was joined by members of both the Randalls' and Cartwrights' congregations. Josiah was laid to rest by a family thankful that his life had not ended with prolonged illness and incapacity. The children agreed that as an invalid, their father would have been impossible to manage.

Over the next few years Madeline continued to garden and make annual trips to visit relatives in Georgia. Yet diabetes was taking its toll, eventually requiring amputation of a leg. She wore the prosthesis well, delighting her church congregation by dancing down the aisle when the choir sang "His Eye Is On the Sparrow." Yet her health had always been problematic, and none of the children were shocked when Madeline's doctor summoned them to discuss their mother's accelerating decline.

As it turned out, Dr. Bailey's verdict would require significant change for all of them. Madeline was going to need help around the clock. Stella spoke up, "But Momma seems to be doing well, she's adjusted to the prosthesis just fine." Dr. Bailey was firm, "Breathing is a struggle for her at times, and her blood pressure drops dangerously low." He was firm in his diagnosis and insistence about her needs.

Stella, Laura, Dimetra, Erica, Harold and Mona sat down and worked out a plan. They would hire a caregiver to attend Madeline during the day, and the siblings would rotate on two-night shifts to stay with her at night, as each of them lived close enough to make this arrangement feasible.

This was the pattern for the next six years. As time passed, the children realized that regular doses of their company were a tonic to Madeline. Her energy increased, her body and spirit seemed renewed. She went fishing more often. She danced more often down the church aisle. There were frequent getaways to Mona's house at Cape May. Over their protests, she even flew to Chicago in a snowstorm for a final visit with her 90 year old brother who was close to death.

It couldn't last forever, of course. Madeline showed

signs of weakening, and her daughters agreed she should live with one of them. The Cartwrights had a three-story house, and Doug was fully agreeable to bringing his mother-in-law there. He ordered installation of a motorized stair lift, which was in progress when he and Mona left for a week-long vacation in the Poconos. In the middle of the night, Laura called with an urgent message, "Momma's had a massive stroke. Dr. Bailey says she's only got six hours to live."

At 3:30 a.m. they started the drive to Chester. Madeline was in a comma when they arrived. Mona learned that her mother had been wrapped in ice the night before to break a high fever. She was horrified to watch her mother's face twist violently as she tried to speak.

When she breathed her last breath, Mona, Erica and Doug were at her bedside. Doug led them in prayer. They sang a hymn, thankful that she was relieved of her pain. In the hospital room and in the days to come, they wept and rejoiced.

For Madeline, there would be no more struggles to breathe, harmony would replace disharmony with Josiah, and all fences would be forgotten and unnecessary. She was at last with the God she loved, whom she had taught her children to love. Mona felt a surge of joy mixed with amusement that much to her surprise, her mother was going to find God considerably more tolerant of foibles, and less judgmental about missteps, than Madeline had ever imagined.

# Chapter Eighteen

## MATURATION IN FAITH

**BIBLE STUDIES REMAINED A** constant part of Mona's life, and helped her through the period of adjustment to her mother's absence. As she made plans to retire from public school teaching, she expressed her intention to get more involved in Bible study at a local AME church. Doug pushed back, encouraging her instead to enroll in seminary where she would receive systematic instruction from knowledgeable professors, versus what he felt where ad hoc and overly simple studies with a fundamentalist orientation. Always a lover of learning, Mona jumped at the idea, especially since the seminary he suggested was Baptist affiliated. Back to her roots! At age 62, she signed up for a Master of Religion course track and started the next phase of her faith maturation journey.

The seminary path proved quite different from anything she had expected. It might be Baptist, but the seminary was far from fundamentalist. She had come thinking her beliefs would be reinforced, but far from it. Ideas she had held since childhood were challenged, one by one. Longstanding convictions about the literalness of scripture were shattered. Mona found the early weeks traumatic, to say the least. Doug was delighted that her "old time religion" perspective was being taken apart, sure that it would be replaced by a deeper and more profound grasp of Biblical truth.

He was right. In time, Mona's sense of spiritual trauma gave way to appreciation and enthusiasm. New vistas opened up and fresh insights came into view. For example, she saw for the first time the scriptural grounding of Episcopal liturgy and appreciated the order of worship as never before.

An Old Testament professor was one of her favorites. "Teach it like it is," he insisted, revealing Old Testament characters with warts and all rather than as mythic heroes. The professor had lived in Japan and sometimes took her to a local Japanese restaurant to continue class discussions. While he opened her mind to scripture, he fell short in teaching her the use of chopsticks.

Much older than any of her classmates, Mona nevertheless made friends easily. On the one hand, she was appalled how the seminary dealt with the loose morals of many young students. One female professor's suggestion to the females for remaining chaste was to pleasure themselves. (A far cry from anything she had heard as an undergraduate at Gatling!) On the other hand, in spite of different ideas about sexual conduct, she became a mentor to several of the young women. One named Helen credited Mona with leading her to Christ. The professors had a lot to teach, Helen said, but not much of it was about following Christ. In contrast, Mona was all about Christ.

In class Mona was an eager participant, full of questions and brave enough to challenge points of view that seemed off base to her. Her knowledge of the Bible and ability to quote scripture verbatim – a practice cultivated since childhood – impressed everyone.

Emotionally, Mona was in a different place than other women in seminary. They tended to be competitive and regard one another as rivals. For a time she led 10 of them in a Wednesday study of Ephesians, but was uncomfortable at the animosity that ran through the group. She suspended the meetings, explaining that there was no "one accordness" among the women. The Holy Spirit wasn't being allowed in.

The same generous impulse she had always felt toward inner city kids, Mona now felt toward some of the seminarians of limited means. Two came from warm locales and weren't prepared for a Philadelphia winter. Mona took them to buy coats and often had them at her house.

For over two years she threw herself into seminary work with all her heart. She would wake up excited and eager to get to class. Mona had continued to teach a Monday night Bible class at her home, and when she introduced some of her seminary learning, she got the same reaction she had felt at first – disorientation, confusion and even alarm. Nonetheless, she persisted, certain that the Lord's hand was guiding the experience.

At the urging of the seminary, she began teaching a Saturday morning community course for preachers who didn't have degrees. They came in large numbers – all ages and from many backgrounds. Many were what her family had always called "jackleg preachers" who maintained that since God told preachers what to say, they didn't need a college degree. Mona knew firsthand the power of tethering God's call to preach to a practice of disciplined study and acquisition of knowledge. She received multiple awards for teaching the course, which continued for two years following her conclusion of seminary. The faculty was delighted that she maintained this role.

Although not required for the degree she was seeking, Mona chose to take a course in Greek so she could read the New Testament in its birth language. The semester-long assignment was to translate the first epistle of John into Greek. Although she didn't pass the course (which did not affect her degree), she never regretted it for the insights it brought. Jesus' comment about hating mother and father stood in a different light once she understood that the sense of the statement was "don't put anyone or anything between you and God."

At age 65, she graduated high in a class of 68 students. Noting her natural counseling skills, faculty members encouraged her to go on for a doctorate in marriage and family counseling. But she feared it could be threatening to Doug if she held a degree of the same level as he held. This decision was a sacrifice for her marriage, because in her heart she wanted to keep going.

After leaving the seminary, Mona stayed close to faculty members as well as some of the young women she had mentored. Five years after she graduated, her family celebrated her 70th birthday at the seminary. All the faculty was invited, delighted to be part of the celebration. For Mona, it was an extraordinary moment – signaling the passage of not just time, but even more of growth in the Lord.

# *Chapter Nineteen*

## PHILIA

**AFTER THEIR MOTHER'S DEATH,** Madeline's daughters were surprised to realize that her departure deprived them of more than they had expected. Like many adult children who become caretakers to their parents, they had found that even in illness, her presence had provided support and reassurance. Her needs forged a bond among them, which quickly dissolved once her care was no longer their united focus. They scattered physically and, to some extent, emotionally.

Stella soon moved to Florida to live with her son. Laura moved to a daughter's home in another part of Pennsylvania. Erica entered an assisted living home in Maryland. Brother Harold moved to Connecticut to be close to his son. Only Dimetra and Mona stayed put, in New Jersey and Philadelphia.

The dispersion bothered Mona. "Why Lord, are we miles from one another at a time such as this? We're getting old, and we should be close to each other to give love and comfort."

Taking the initiative to keep family ties strong, Mona began the practice of making annual trips in the spring and fall to visit her sisters. With Stella, Laura and even Erica, the visits went well. Mona and Stella would stay up late, laughing, eating and reminiscing, and go to bed still giggling. Laura would plan elaborate meals, outlining her plans for the next sumptuous dinner even as they were still at the table eating the present one. Erica also seemed happy to see her whenever she came, although sharing remained a bit awkward between them.

Visits to Dimetra were another matter. Wherever or whenever she got together with family, Dimetra wanted the occasion to be "family only." On one particular trip, she resented that Mona planned lunch with one of her former teacher colleagues. The two had taught together for ten years and become fast friends. That meant little to Dimetra. "You're supposed to be coming to see me, but you're spending your time with that woman," she blurted out in reproach.

As Dimetra's rant continued, Mona answered, "I think you're being a bit unreasonable. I've traveled a long way to be with you, hoping that our time together would be filled with fun and scrabble."

Dimetra shot back, "No one forces you to come, and I don't need that money you leave." (On each visit to a sibling, Mona always left an envelope of cash for them to find after she left.)

"The money is a gift of love," Mona answered. "I'm so sorry that we have to spend part of our time in this bickering way."

In spite of Dimetra's caustic hospitality, Mona continued to tuck an envelope under the placemat where her sister would be sure to find it.

As time passed, Mona's role changed from youngest sister to mother hen. She would bring her sisters together in the Pocono Mountains, choosing times when she felt that God was "showing off" his creative excellence in beautifying the world. But instead of promoting cohesion among them, being together in this way sometimes had the opposite effect. Brief times of pleasantries – playing games, sharing delicious meals – were offset, at least to Mona, by omissions. To her, they were experiencing their last opportunities to reflect on times past and tell each other, "I'm sorry" and "I was wrong" and "Please forgive me."

As Mona long had realized, the Randall sisters had never been inclined to such expressions, and age seemed to harden that fact. Mona had no doubt that each of her sisters had faith in God, yet she often felt that they had neglected to become anchored in his Word regarding love and forgiveness. She continued bringing them together as often as she could, visiting them yearly and leaving the little stashes of money that were her way of saying, "I love you and always will."

*\*\**

With Harold, things were different. Mona's spiritual awakening had brought her into a more meaningful relationship with her brother than the two had ever enjoyed in their younger years.

Although closest to each other in age as well as the two youngest of the Randall children, growing up they had often been at odds. As the only boy, Harold had felt a sense of entitlement. Mona, the baby, had always been coddled and spoiled. Clashes where inevitable, and the emotional distance between them lingered into adulthood. Yet time and circumstances paved the way for a fresh start between the siblings.

Now they could laugh about childhood spats. Whenever Mona had found herself on the losing end of an argument, she would bring their father into the fray. "Poppa, Harold's feet smell," Mona would complain. "Boy, go wash your feet," Josiah would respond. Harold would protest that his feet were fine; he had just taken a bath. But once Josiah gave an order, he wasn't backing off. "I said go wash your feet, and I meant go wash your feet." So Harold would trudge off to fetch water to boil on the pot belled stove, feeling no affection for his little sister.

As a youth, Harold had been a handful for all his sisters other than Erica. She had him wrapped around her finger, as she did so many others. With his remaining four sisters, including Mona, Harold angered easily and was always determined to have the last word in any disagreement. The notion of apologizing for an insult never occurred to him. When he brought friends home, they rarely were of a type his mother would have chosen for him. Beyond the fence, Harold and his buddies often got into trouble, although usually of a minor nature.

In his teen years, he showed a gift for electrical work and by age 18 was well established as the neighborhood's favorite electrician. Around this time he also fell deeply in love with a young woman he met at church. Celeste was soft spoken and shy, yet she clearly returned his affectionate feelings.

Madeline was having none of it, because Celeste had a two year old child born out of wedlock. "Harold, you know you can't fool with that girl," she insisted.
"But Momma, she's a good person and I really love her," he pleaded.

Madeline's sense of propriety in matters related to sexual behavior outweighed all other considerations. "Sometimes we have to give up what we want if we're going to do the right thing," she said firmly.

Although Harold's sisters were all very fond of Celeste and believed that marrying her was the right thing for their brother to do, Madeline showed an iron will which prevailed. Sadly, Harold broke off the relationship. As the years passed, Mona came to believe he never really got over this powerful first love.
A few years later he met Anna, whose mother had hired him for electrical work. Anna set her sights on the energetic young man immediately, and they married soon

after. His new wife's family was well educated and were involved in a range of professional ventures. Harold felt pressured to rise to their standard of living. The couple moved to an affluent neighborhood. As four children came on the scene, Anna had a part-time maid to help.

In spite of his successful business, Harold also had a longtime passion for aviation. He enlisted in the Air Force and was frequently away from home. At the time of his discharge, he decided to surprise Anna by showing up unannounced and letting her know that his Air Force days were over. But it was Harold who got the surprise. When he walked in the house, a strange man was seated with Anna at the dinner table. The stranger hurriedly left, but the context of the situation left no doubt about why he was there.

"How long have you been seeing this guy?" Harold angrily asked Anna. She was unrepentant, answering, "You're gone all the time and when you're home, you're always busy putting holes in somebody's wall. I get lonesome! What do you want me to do?"

From that point, their quarreling intensified. Anna seemed to take pleasure in informing Harold that she had had lovers before they married, and he suspected the stranger at dinner might not be her only adulterous affair. Soon they were making divorce arrangements.

Mona felt for her brother. He had given up the love of his life out of loyalty to his mother. His rebound marriage had crumbled in spite of his devotion to Anna. After the break-up with Anna his children stayed close to their father and spent much time with the Randalls at the Reaney Street home.

On top of domestic heartbreak, his Air Force experience had been disappointing as he fell short of qualifying to become a pilot. With discouragements piling up, he threw caution to the wind and assumed a "Casanova" lifestyle. Before long he met and married Clarice, a much younger woman whom Harold's sisters quickly sized up as being mainly interested in his wallet.

Clarice was more devious than they imagined. One afternoon as Harold was napping, he awoke suddenly to see his wife standing over him with a large kitchen knife pointed at his heart. She thrust it downward as he bolted upward. Because of his quick move, she missed vital organs and blood vessels. He was gashed in the chest and bled heavily.
In the aftermath, Harold refused to involve the police – which disappointed but did not surprise Mona. That was

her brother's way. Soon it came to light that Clarice's motive had been a modest life insurance policy he owned. After one thwarted love and two disappointing marriages, Harold's chances at finding a fulfilling relationship with a true kindred spirit seemed slim. But God had better plans. (Jeremiah 29:11)

Throughout his time of living with careless abandon, he stayed connected to his church and even continued mentoring youth. Thus he crossed paths with Ava, a member of the church choir and Sunday School teacher for preschoolers. A lifelong nurse, Ava had three grown daughters and five beautiful grandchildren. Her husband, a deacon in the church, had died three years earlier.

A person of few words, Ava let her smile and gracious demeanor define who she was. Harold, on the other hand, was quick to speak up. "The Lord has told me you will be my wife," he whispered to her one snowy morning as she exited church.

Ava was startled. "I don't even know you! Why are you saying this?"

Harold was ready with an answer. "I know you don't know me, and I want to change that."

Piqued at having her privacy invaded, Ava was impervious to his charm. "Sorry, but I'm not the least bit interested in you or anyone else. Where did you get the notion that God gave you such a ridiculous idea?" She walked hastily to her car and drove off.

Harold felt that this first advance to Ava had not gone as badly as he feared it might. He set about in earnest to win her: phone calls, letters, flowers and more attempts to engage her in conversation. It took nine months of courting, but they were finally joined in holy wedlock at the church altar, just a short distance from where he first spoke to her of his intentions.

They moved to his apartment, and Ava quickly became an integral part of the Randall family. Harold's sisters adored her, and Madeline finally had someone who, like herself, never tired of playing scrabble.

Harold's finding of happiness with Ava coincided with Mona's experience of being born again. He was the only Randall sibling who was fascinated by the event and its aftermath. Like an inquisitive child he asked Mona over and over to recount her salvation story. A spiritual connection between them developed, bringing each one great joy as they shared their ideas about holy scripture. Health problems had forced Harold to give up his electrician business, and he now supplemented his income as a part-time travel agent. When finances for her brother got tight, Mona and Doug provided assistance. Harold and Ava began to spend considerable time with the Cartwrights, and Mona was pleased to see that a congenial relationship was emerging between her husband and brother.

Affection between sister and brother was especially evident on Mona's 70th birthday. At a party in her honor, Harold surprised his sister by reading to the assembled guests a letter he had composed for Mona.

*Mona, I love you dearly. God has blessed us to draw very close, through Him, in our last few years.*

*God's promise in the 5th commandment – Honor thy father and thy mother that thy days may be long upon the land which the Lord thy God has given thee. We did honor and respect our very strict parents and as God promised, we have lived long and you have reached 70 years old, the last of Momma and Poppa's six children.*

*Let's reminisce for a few moments. Do you remember when we made mud pies, grass dolls and waited for our special chicken to lay eggs, then rung their heads off and cooked them? Remember the few times we got the switch for taking and eating forbidden fruit from our neighbor's trees? Remember our weekly Saturday baths in a tin laundry tub? Remember how mischievous you were – and still are – with your little tricks played especially on me, getting me in trouble with Poppa? Then there was that time when Momma was chiding us and said, 'You children just don't count me,' and you retorted, 'Momma, I count you, 1,2,3,4,5.'*

*And what about the time when Erica would say 'absolutely' and I would say 'positively' and you would chime in with the word 'conductor' which was the largest word you knew at the time.*

*But mischievous as you were – and will remain – you were just as brilliant, being twice double promoted, and you and I entered junior high school together. We studied together and enjoyed many pleasant times, like going to the Roxy Theater, playing baseball in the streets, picking blackberries and going to Woodside Park.*

*Mona I could go on and on through the years, but now to the crowning point of your life – Jesus! You love our Lord. You and Brother Doug have fed the hungry, given drink to the thirsty, clothed the naked, visited the sick and ministered to the imprisoned, both materially and spiritually. You have been mother and father to a host of children, housing, feeding and clothing them. You dared to talk about God and His love in your classroom throughout your years of teaching. Your resources have been made available to all who were in need, and even I have been a recipient of your generosity.*

*You have 'studied to make yourself approved unto God, a workman that needeth not to be ashamed, rightly dividing the word of truth. 2nd Timothy 2:15*

*We have grown close together in these last few years. We are of one accord through Jesus Christ our Lord. These segments of our lives with each other are cherished memories. I love you, Sister by human blood and the blood of our Lord and Savior, Jesus Christ. You are a friend, mentor and a true servant of God. I love you very dearly and thank God for the blessing you are in my life."*

Harold's letter touched Mona deeply. It focused her thoughts on the journey each of them had traveled from the humble home of their childhood on Reaney Street, through the twisting path of adulthood, to the season of peace that age brings. Each had enjoyed professional success and, in spite of hurdles, had come to know the blessings of a harmonious marriage. As young children they had been rivals and often were thorns in each other's sides. Now each appreciated the other as never before.

Yet just when life seemed to be fully on track for Harold at last, illness intervened. He was diagnosed with prostate cancer. To Mona's alarm, he declined medical help in the belief that God would heal him. Meanwhile Ava was diagnosed with ovarian cancer. In spite of her long nursing career, she deliberately allowed the disease to go untreated, confessing to Mona that she didn't want to be on earth without Harold. As his prostate cancer had advanced, he also developed ALS. Ava cared for Harold as long as she could, passing away six months before he did.

To Mona, a wonderful Cinderella story had needlessly turned into a Romeo and Juliet tragedy. She was angry that both had chosen to die out of their time, or so it seemed to her.

Yet she cherished the reconnection with Harold and the time they had spent sharing spiritual matters. She also was grateful to know that her brother, so long beset by anger and relationship troubles, in the end had experienced both deep human love and the unconditional love of God.

# Chapter Twenty

## MIGRATION SOUTH

**MONA HAD SPENT THE** first two decades of her life firmly planted in one place, Reaney Street in Chester. In the many years since leaving her parents' home for college, she had become accustomed to moving on a frequent basis. It was part of being married to a priest whose organizational talents resulted in numerous assignments to found new churches or stabilize and rejuvenate failing congregations.

She and Doug had raised their family mostly in Episcopal rectories in working class neighborhoods. Congregants had sometimes encouraged Mona to expose the children to the "best people" by involving them in prestigious activities like the Jack and Jill Club. She and Doug were determined to steer their family clear of associations that seemed elitist and to discourage exclusive impulses. This was not hard, since the nature of all three children was to reach out, include and look for ways to be helpful. Miriam, Adam and Priscilla attended public school throughout their elementary and secondary years. In adulthood, they fulfilled their parents hopes of being grounded, well educated and community-minded young adults. With family responsibilities of their own, each concluded that staying in Philadelphia did not offer their best opportunity. One by one, they left, and they all wound up in the same place, Atlanta. Two generations after their grandparents had joined the great migration north, the Cartwright children were part of a move in the opposite direction.

Priscilla was the first to go. She had been working as a medical clinic receptionist in 1985 when her job was terminated. Undertaking a strategically astute employment search, she joined The Center for Innovative Training and Education (CITE), a federal training program that provided students with money for transportation, lunch and day care for their children. After six months of training, Priscilla and her spouse of 20 years relocated to Atlanta where she became CITE's project director. Thriving in her new home town, within five years Priscilla was offered the position of Vice President of Education at the Metro Atlanta Chamber of Commerce, the first African American to hold the position in the organization's 133 year history. She subsequently became a prominent figure in Atlanta philanthropy as Senior Vice President of the Community Foundation for Greater Atlanta.

Within a year of her younger sister leaving Philadelphia, Miriam followed Priscilla to Atlanta. She was now a single mother with three children to support, and she felt that she could make better use of her PhD in mental health in a new environment. Her expectations bore fruit. Earning a Master's of Divinity degree from Emory University's Candler School of Theology, she became CEO of a powerful prison ministry, Women in Transition. She also married a loving, devoted husband, experiencing God's graciousness in both career and family life.

Adam, father of two sons and a daughter, also came to Atlanta to advance his career in graphic arts. The scope of his interests included drawing, printing, writing and photography. His first magazine, FORWARD, was done in a vivid lifestyle format that drew immediate response from the public. His other passion was mountain living, and he led a construction crew that built homes around Cherokee, Tennessee. He also had a real estate career focused on Atlanta's growing suburbs.

A sequence of illnesses for Mona and Doug caused their children to travel often to Philadelphia. First Doug had a throat infection that led to surgery for tonsillitis. Soon after, Mona was advised to have a hysterectomy. When the surgery proved lengthier than expected, she was administered a drug that provoked a severe allergic reaction. Not since the internal injuries of the automobile accident had Mona been so close to death. As she recovered, she and Doug acknowledged to each other that they had reached an age in which proximity to the children held advantages for everyone. Yet they resisted pulling up stakes.

On their next trip to Atlanta, several of the granddaughters gathered around Mona and implored her to move to Atlanta. They wanted their grandparents to be part of their lives on a regular basis, not just for occasional visits. Their pleas carried the day.

Doug was close to retirement. They already had sold the Cape May property while Mona was in seminary and purchased a condo in the city. On a hectic wintry day shortly before Christmas, Doug was in Philadelphia to close on the sale of the condo. Mona was in Atlanta for the closing on their new house. As they celebrated the New Year with their beloved children and grands,

Mona and Doug looked forward to settling into a family-centered life.

Yet, they soon doubted they had made the right decision. More than expected, they missed their Philadelphia friends and familiar routines. Mona loved the house they bought, situated on a big corner lot with lovely trees. But she was lonely and could tell that Doug was too. Then a friend of Miriam's introduced them to an organization called the Quality Living Services located not far from their home. From that point, everything changed.

The Center became their connection to new friends and a host of interests, new and old. Long time bridge players, Mona and Doug both resumed the game with gusto. Mona took a class in floral arranging. They got their first taste of computer study and both soon were hooked. The Center hosted interesting speakers and services for various senior needs. And the lunches were delicious. Soon Mona was volunteering for the Center and wound up as president of the board of directors. She went to work on fundraising, both to expand into new activities and to retire the organization's debt, and her efforts made a major impact.

Other interests blossomed as well, including travel. At least Mona was interested – Doug preferred staying put, having taken an adjunct teaching position in sociology at Morehouse College.

While living in Philadelphia Mona had visited the Holy Land on a tour sponsored by evangelist Pat Robertson (and played cards with his son on the plane). She also had enjoyed Caribbean cruises with several faith-based groups. In Atlanta she became a true world traveler, sometimes accompanied by her daughters. She returned to Europe and made trips to South Africa and several West African nations. With various service groups she visited Japan, China and Hong Kong and traveled with a youth organization to Latin America. Within the US she saw more of the country than ever before in her travels to see family and to play in bridge tournaments.

At home, she and Doug were pleased that old friends came through Atlanta often, and the Cartwrights loved to entertain them. Meeting several neighbors who shared her interest in Bible study, Mona started a community group that met weekly to explore the scriptures. The Cartwrights also had become members of an Episcopal Church in the community. This was very familiar landscape, of course, and they were instantly embraced by the congregation.

When the parish priest of the past 20 years left, Doug was called by the bishop to serve as interim priest for six months. It was the perfect match of servant and situation. For one last time, his organizing and pastoral skills were applied to good use. Already well liked, Doug and Mona came to occupy a place of deep affection and appreciation within the church. An extra blessing for the Cartwrights was the close friendship they developed with the rector who later became the bishop of Atlanta and his family during this time.

Soon after the new priest arrived and Doug was relieved of further responsibilities, Mona began to notice a decline in his health. Already he had given up his teaching position at Morehouse. For years he had contended with diabetes, leading to several urinary tract surgeries. Now his stamina was weakening, and he struggled to climb stairs, convincing Mona they needed to find a smaller, single-level home. Miriam offered the ideal solution in her own spacious home – a lovely in-law apartment with a yard that overlooked a wooded hillside.

Even though this move appeared to be the perfect answer, it was a sacrifice for Mona. She would sorely miss her neighborhood Bible study group and her beautiful yard where they often entertained with a big tent in the back yard. Mona loved the magnificent crepe myrtles, magnolias, Leyland cypresses and the roses she had planted, yet she felt the Holy Spirit telling her that moving was the right thing to do. She responded to the push, keenly aware that she and Doug were going to their last home.

# *Chapter Twenty-One*

## LAST DANCE

**AS THE CARTWRIGHTS SETTLED** into life in the apartment, Mona found a new favorite place in the world. The apartment had a large and well shaded screened porch, situated with a pleasant view of the backyard garden and woods beyond. A gentle breeze often stirred the Corinthian chimes she had hung. Any time of day she might be found there - reading, writing notes, adding entries to her journal or reflecting on the winding path that had started so long ago on Reaney Street, and led to this spot.

She thought of creature comforts now taken for granted, but once unheard of. How her mother had heated an iron on the pot-bellied stove to warm the bed in winter. How the explosive sounds that old stove sometimes released had startled her from sleep in the night. For perhaps the thousandth time in her life, Mona felt gratitude and wonder that her family had never suffered a fire from sparks flying from the stove's chimney.

Although Doug didn't have to exert himself as much as in their former home, his health was not improving. He no longer went out except for doctor appointments and one Sunday a month when he accompanied Mona to church. Increasingly he fretted whenever she left the house without him. This happened often, as Mona's calendar remained full of activities, from church to the senior center to outings with friends. She also still traveled occasionally, to visit one of her sisters, see friends in Philadelphia, or attend the annual Cartwright reunion of Doug's extended family.

In these circumstances Mona arranged for professional care-givers or family members to stay with Doug, but invariably he begged her not to leave. Only her presence would satisfy him. This was a dilemma. Mona had no thought of becoming housebound, especially when there were plenty of appropriate options to assure his safety and well-being. But he would have none of it.

Miriam, with her psychological training, diagnosed

depression as the root cause of her father's Mona-dependence. She had heard of a senior depression treatment program at a local university and investigated it along with Priscilla. It was a group-based therapy program which emphasized socializing with others. Convinced it could help Doug, they encouraged him to enroll. He balked but they persisted.

Once he began participating, the change in his spirit was dramatic. Mona could hardly believe the enthusiasm he showed. His neediness for her constant presence subsided. When she left him for outings or travel, he was content with the care-givers she arranged. Best of all, the positive effects didn't disappear once he finished the program. It was a miracle, she thankfully told her daughters.

The change was timely, because she was eager to visit her sisters while she still could. Stella already had passed away. She had lived for some years with her son in Florida, and Mona felt compassion for him because Stella had become needy and demanding. In her last days, her daughter came to live with her.

Dimetra's gardening and cooking talents remained undiminished as her years advanced. She became forgetful, however, sometimes unable to find her way back home in the car. When she had surgery for a stomach tumor, Mona, Laura and Erica all went to be with her. The visit turned into a party, as the sisters once again had fun together sharing memories and going on outings while Dimetra recovered.

Four years later, the malignancy returned. "I won't make it this time," Dimetra confided to Laura, who passed the word on to Mona. When Dimetra died, Mona was with her daughter Gale at her bedside in the hospital room. In those last minutes, it seemed to Mona that Dimetra was trying to tell her something but couldn't make herself understood. Mona strongly suspected it had something to do with an argument between Dimetra and Laura, with Dimetra wanting Mona to take her side. What a way to depart, Mona thought.

All her adult life, Mona had looked forward to her visits with Laura, the family historian. Somehow, Laura had learned secrets and tidbits that no one else seemed to know. When her 90th birthday was approaching, her children planned a Roaring 20s party. Family members came from far and wide, to sing, dance and celebrate. Laura, in a gorgeous outfit her children had bought, sat at a table, unusually quiet.

Mona had been aware that her sister wasn't feeling well

but had no idea how sick she was until back home after the party, when Laura fell across her bed and told Mona, "I can't make it anymore."

One of Laura's daughters was an RN, married to a doctor. They immediately took Laura to the hospital, where she was admitted. Tests showed that she had leukemia. She spent a week in the hospitals receiving transfusions. After she was released the transfusions continued periodically, until Laura declined to have any more because they made her feel worse than the leukemia. In effect, "she pulled her own plug," Mona told others. "She said she was through with all that." Laura lived another two years before succumbing to her illness.

Erica's last years were especially sad to Mona. Her decline had begun with a fall in her apartment, and it was the next day before she was found on her kitchen floor. Permanently crippled, she went to live with her daughter and son-in-law. The house was large but there was no downstairs bedroom. To get to her room, Erica had to work her way up the stairs in a manner that made Mona think of a snake slithering. Reaching the top of the stairs, she would lurch toward her son-in-law who was positioned to catch her. To Mona's wonder, Erica boasted about her ability to manage this feat. But soon, she lost even this mobility. Mona's last visit with her was in a nursing home, and Erica died soon after.

As the only surviving Randall sibling, it occurred to Mona that all her sisters had lived well beyond their "threescore and ten" Biblical allotment of years. Harold, too, had lived into his 70s. Mona was now in her 80s, experiencing a remarkable state of good health that surpassed them all. Meanwhile, Doug's decline was accelerating. Mona fixed meals that she knew were his favorites, but it seemed he had less appetite with each passing day. It was winter, and she sensed that his time was growing short. She wondered if he would be able to join her on the porch to take joy in the new spring growth emerging in the yard. When Doug stopped eating completely, Adam insisted on taking his father to the doctor, an internist who knew him well. Immediately on seeing Doug, she exclaimed over his color. "You're yellow!" Her examination was brief, and she ordered an ambulance to transport him directly to the hospital.

There was little doubt among the Cartwrights that bad news was coming. After extensive tests, the family and a few close friends had gathered at his bedside to learn the doctor's report. Indeed it was grim. Doug had pancreatic cancer, already in an advanced stage. No treatment was indicated.

Across the years there had been only a few occasions when Mona and Doug discussed death in a personal way. He had been clear about his wishes. "I don't want to die any sooner than I have to," he told her consistently. "Put tubes in me, keep me going as long as possible." Mona always had assumed he had a deep fear of death, but now he was stoic.

"I'm going home to die," he told his loved ones. "I know Mona will be all right. She is provided for, and the children will see to her well-being." Then Doug fell silent, profoundly so. It was apparent he had nothing more to say. Adam, standing beside Mona, asked his mother, "Do you want to say anything Mommy?" She had no words, only the strength to put her arms around Doug and weep. At home in those final days, Mona never was far from his bedside, although a practical nurse also was there to attend to him during the day. Children and grandchildren were often present, including out-of-town grandchildren who came to tell him a final goodbye.

One morning Mona walked outside with departing visitors when she heard the nurse summon her back. "Come in, he wants you." Mona could hear Doug's voice as she approached the bedroom. "Mona, Mona come here," he called. "I'm right here, Doug I'm right here," she assured him. But he was beyond knowing who was near, or what was going on. Even as she put her arms around him and held him, he kept calling, "Mona, Mona, come here."

She called the bishop who had grown so close to them and asked that he arrange for last rites. He came himself later that day, along with their parish priest and two others. After the clergy had left, Mona lingered in the garden. It was a mild late afternoon, although the calendar had just turned to March. She knew that death was close at hand, yet all around her, life was renewing itself and new beauty would soon emerge. Within a few hours, Doug was gone.

A magnificent funeral mass was celebrated, with the bishop officiating. The cathedral was filled, including many friends from Philadelphia and other points along the way of his priesthood. Mona and the children knew how beloved he had been by many people. Yet it often happens upon a death that the closest family learns with surprise how far was the reach of their loved one, how many lives were touched, how much good had been done without their awareness. So it was with the Cartwrights. After the interment, family and friends returned to Mona's home for a meal and to continue visiting and sharing memories. Mona had memories that were hers alone – joyful and painful. She realized that their journey together had taken many turns, over many years, before the two had really come to understand each other. And to understand themselves.

As a couple, Mona and Doug had traveled a difficult path to reach a point of true knowledge as well as deep love. This made everything worthwhile. Now, in very different ways, each was at peace. Guests filled her living room, speaking in the solemn tones fit for such a time. "Let's push back the furniture," Mona announced. "I want to dance." And they did!

# Chapter Twenty-two

## CHRISTMAS SPIRIT

**IN THE MONTH'S FOLLOWING** Doug's death, Mona felt that she was adjusting to the loss in a healthy way. She resumed old routines and established some new ones, highlighted by family events, church activities, book club meetings, weekly Bridge sessions, correspondence with friends and relatives and, of course, her daily devotional practice. At the end of the year, the holidays came and went – Christmas, Kwanzaa and New Years – and she experienced the same feelings as always, appreciation and joy. "I guess I did my grieving while he was dying," she decided, remembering the countless tears that flowed as she watched his struggles.

The second holiday season without him brought very

different emotions, and a strong unease about being alone. She began to reflect on how little of her life she had spent extensive time alone. From childhood she had been surrounded by a large family. As an adult, there was an expanded family, plus friends whom once made, she held fast in spite of relocations.

Now solitude as her lot, was both painful and irritating. Instead of missing Doug less with the passing of time, she found that his absence hurt more. She still enjoyed people and activity and anticipated both with pleasure. Yet there were moments when melancholy would fall over her – never more so than on the second Christmas Day after his passing.

Before Christmas, she had been filled with expectancy, looking forward to gatherings with friends and family and especially the busy schedule at church. Mona delighted in the worship service at which the younger generation presented a remarkable welcoming of the Christ Child, including chorale works, solos, recitations and instrumental performances. It was an invitation to relive the awesome thrill of the Incarnation, the birth of the Lord, through spoken word and music. It was also an affirmation that a new generation was carrying forward the Holy message. She had been deeply moved.

Then came Christmas Day. The plan was for family members to gather at her home in late afternoon. Mona had been invited by each of her children to join them as they visited in-laws earlier in the day, but she had feared it would wear her out, so she declined. As a result, she spent most of Christmas Day alone, which proved more taxing than accompanying the children. She was despondent – so much so that she went back to bed – an extremely rare event for her. As 5 p.m. approached, she got up to dress, but her rest had not been refreshing. If anything, she was more dispirited than before.

Her mood did not lighten as people began to arrive. With each new wave of guests, there were joyous greetings and exchanges of affection. As the house grew more crowded, and the merriment compounded, Mona realized that a deep depression had taken hold of her. She had no desire to participate in the gaiety, but didn't want to alarm her guests by retiring, or offend them by yawning. She sat quietly in a rocker, waving to incoming visitors, avoiding all but the most surface conversations, trying hard not to nod off.

No one seemed to notice except Adam. "Momma, are you all right?" he asked. "Yes, Adam, I'm fine," she fibbed. He didn't give up the subject. "It's not like you to be so quiet with all these people around," he said. "Maybe getting old has something to do with it," she answered. "And I've always felt a bit low after experiencing an enormously joyful time."

Adam offered to make her a cup of coffee or tea, and she agreed to a cup of black coffee. "Maybe that will wake me up," she said. As Adam left the room, the doorbell rang again. It was Esther, mother-in-law of one of Mona's granddaughters, who had come down from Cincinnati. In the ten years since Athena had married Clyde, Esther and Mona had become fast friends. Now Esther arrived with another son Marvin and grandson Jacob. After greeting each other, the two women settled in a quiet corner of the family room.

After a few minutes Mona was unable to stifle a yawn, and Esther was sympathetic. "You need to go to bed. I'm keeping you up." Embarrassed, Mona moved from a rocking chair to the leather sofa beside Esther. "Oh, I'm sorry to be so rude, but I had planned to take a power nap just before the doorbell rang. Please forgive me."

As the conversation continued, Esther's part of it was falling on nearly deaf ears – literally. Mona was learning to accept the fact that her hearing was progressively less acute. She could be actively engaged in a discussion, then lose its direction. Her hearing aids were becoming less effective. Rather than being drawn back into the conversation, Mona changed the subject to the sweet potato pie that was Esther's dinner contribution.

"It looks delicious," said Mona. "Shall we try it?"

Esther replied, "Yes, I'd like a piece. My neighbor in Cincinnati makes the best pies ever, and it's her recipe. I was hoping y'all would like it."

As they were cutting the pie, several of Mona's great grandchildren burst through the door, looking for a hiding place as they played hide and seek. "Enough already!" Mona exclaimed to them. "It's nearly midnight."

Esther herded the children out. "You'll have to go back upstairs with your grandmother. Granny is exhausted, and your screaming is giving me a terrible headache." At the same time, she and Marvin moved toward the door to leave.

Mona protested, "Esther that demand wasn't aimed at you."

"I know," Esther replied, "but you need to go to bed anyway."

As they left, Mona sat on the sofa, so tired she could hardly move, regretting that the visit with Esther had been disrupted. Her 92nd Christmas Day had been uniquely unsatisfying. Mona was thankful she could look ahead to Kwanzaa and New Years in the hope that they would revive her mood and redeem the keen sense of God's presence that always defined the season for her.

***

She celebrated Kwanzaa in the Tennessee mountains with Adam and his wife Elise. They had built the retreat house nearly 20 years ago, and Mona had spent many happy hours there. Kwanzaa was always a highlight, as Elise prepared dinner for 20 guests. She combined southern dishes with Caribbean offerings of jerky chicken, beans and rice, plantains, potato salad flavored with beets, and other delights from her native Trinidad. Everyone ate with gusto.

The Kwanzaa message "Nia" meant purpose, challenging the hearers to strive more diligently for meaning and purpose in the coming year. Most of the attendees participated in the service with pledges, singing and dancing. Younger ones in the group were awed by the solemnity of the devotionals. Games went on until 4 a.m.

Even the youngest remained awake and alert long after retiring.

Mona slept until 10 the next morning, then donned her robe and joined grandson Changa and his step-daughter Maria, age 16, who had Down syndrome. Her attention instantly was fixed on Maria's leopard print pajamas, so similar to her own. Mona already knew that Maria shared her passion for the color purple, right down to the purple cases that protected their respective cell phones. She also knew that their birthdays were just four days apart. Coincidences or something else?

Excusing herself, Mona retired to her room for prayer and meditation. She sought guidance as to whether the Lord was using these small signs to convey His will on a larger matter.Returning to the kitchen she sat down with Changa and Maria, blessed the meal and asked Maria to accept her as her godmother. With tears of joy, Maria ran into her arms.

****

New Year's Day brought to Mona's mind the promise of God recorded in Jeremiah 29, "For I know the plans I have for you ..." Priscilla and Benjamin had long planned their 40th anniversary on the first day of year, to be celebrated with a throng of friends and loved ones. As the day approached, however, a mysterious intuition had led Priscilla to cancel the 60 "save the day" notices she had sent out. It was a prescient move, as one week before the day, Benjamin got word from his brother in Erie, Pennsylvania that their mother had been rushed to the hospital with a heart attack and was in critical condition. Miriam decided to host a different type of anniversary event with a diminished guest list. Attendees greeted Priscilla with "Happy New Year, God bless you for many more." Prayer circles formed spontaneously during the gathering to give praise and thanks, ask travel mercies for Benjamin, God's hand on his mother and the family attending her, and to offer a variety of special requests.

As guests were leaving, they chuckled as Miriam sent each one forth with a bag of fried chicken. The store from which she had ordered had "over-sent" by $100 worth and could not accept the returned surplus. Thus on her 40th anniversary, Priscilla had celebrated in the company of close friends as well as family – all of them focused on providing love and support for the need of the moment. Later than evening, word came from Benjamin that his mother's condition had stabilized, and she was being transferred from ICU to a hospital room. The anniversary couple made plans for an island getaway when Benjamin returned.

The gathering and its aftermath held tremendous significance for Mona. In the year's first assembling of this loving, close-knit group, the Divine presence was among them anointing and blessing. She pondered the revival of her own spirit since Christmas Day just one week earlier, and gave thanks for the ongoing evidence she saw and felt of Emmanuel – God With Us.

*Epilogue*

## PEACEABLE PORCH

**MONA WOKE WITH A** start, having dozed off while reading on the porch.  Her eyes fell on the large-print Bible she had bought Doug years before when his eye sight was failing.  As she picked it up, the book fell open to Zephaniah 3:17: "The Lord your God is in your midst.  The mighty One will save.  He will rejoice over you with gladness.  He will quiet you with His love."

Peace fell over her like a blanket, which often happened as she sat on the porch.  She viewed her porch as "an island of peace within one's soul; well within the island is the temple where God dwells.  This is the place where there is no pretense, to dishonesty, no adulteration." (Howard Thurman's "Meditations of the Heart.)  The surrounding trees, flowers, birds and animals added to the sacredness of her sanctum.

The quiet porch with its lovely view took her thoughts back to a different porch many years earlier, with a busier, more crowded scene. On that long-ago porch, she had been surrounded by noise – Randall family voices in conversations, outbursts of laughter, children playing games, and the crackle of the mosquito-repelling smudge pot.

That porch on Reaney Street also had symbolized refuge to her. Inside the house, there were sibling quarrels, her mother's unending list of "do nots" and her father's frequent harsh words to his wife and children alike. Out in the yard, there was a fence to warn of a foreboding world beyond. On the porch, there was safe and calm middle ground where arguments were set aside and good fellowship prevailed.

Now this screened porch of her late years was a safe space, too – for a host of memories, reflections on the here-and-now, and imaginative journeys into the future. Preparing for whatever the day would bring, she prayed each morning A Prayer of Self Dedication from the Book of Common Prayer page 832:

"Almighty and eternal God, so draw our hearts to thee, so guide our minds, so fill our imaginations, so control our wills, that we may be wholly thine, utterly dedicated unto thee; and then use us, we pray thee, as thou wilt, and always to thy glory and the welfare of thy people, through our Lord and Savior Jesus Christ. Amen"

She was on the porch one afternoon when a sudden burst of rain came down on a sunny sky. Mona exclaimed with a laugh, "The devil's beating his wife!" How many times in her youth had she heard her mother say this in similar conditions? "Madeline's Almanac" was chock-full of such aphorisms. "If your palm itches, you're going to get money from an unknown source. Spill the salt, expect bad luck. Close all the doors and drawers before you get into bed."

Mona smiled to recall that to her mother, superstitions were vividly real. Madeline had passed them on to Mona and all her children with emphasis!

The memories brought to mind Franciscan monk Richard Rohr's description of the "second half of life" in his book, *Falling Upwards.* Mona realized she had long been there, spiritually as well as physically. She nodded as she read Rohr's words, "Most of us tend to think of the second half of life as largely about getting old, dealing with health issues and letting go of our physical life. But what looks like falling can largely be experienced as falling upward and onward into a broader and deeper world where the soul has found its fullness, is finally connected to the whole and lives inside the Big Picture. It is not a loss but somehow a gain, not losing but actually winning."

In this vein, Mona had much to ponder from a recent visit with family and old friends in the North. Received like a beloved matriarch, Mona had found nieces and nephews, as well as former students, in various states of readiness to embrace the second half of life. She gave much thought to how she might nudge each of them toward the fullness she felt, and wanted them to experience.

At least one of them was already there, Mona felt sure. Her niece Gail, Dimetra's only child, had become a kindred spirit of Mona's some time ago. They had grown close as Dimetra was dying when Gail had shared a telling memory from a Randall family reunion long ago. On a bus trip through Amish country, most of the family had been appalled at the recklessness of the driver. Gail, a teen at the time, was outright frightened. But as the bus had sped over a hill, Gail had heard Mona laugh and say, "Ohhh, a roller coaster!" At these words, Gail's fear eased and changed to enjoyment. The moment had stayed with her, and thereafter she looked to Mona as a model for enjoying life as it came.

Mona was sure this had not been easy in Gail's relations with her mother. She knew all too well how caustic her sister could be and had no doubt that her acrid tongue had wounded Gail more than once. As Dimetra showed signs of memory loss, Gail had encouraged her to come live in her home. Dimetra had been particularly ungracious in declining – "I would go crazy living in the house with those four children," she told her daughter.

After the time they shared as Dimetra was dying, Mona and Gail grew increasingly close. Gail never failed to remember her aunt on holidays and her birthday. She wrote her letters, one of which touched Mona deeply. "How you handle life's problems is indicative of a child of God who is most loved by Him. You have a very important role in my life."

Affirmations in the same spirit came from students whom Mona had taught or gotten to know during her seminary studies. She had become a mentor to several young female seminarians and kept close to three of them through later years. Constance, more often called Connie, was tall, thin and blonde with sparkling blue eyes. Mona had come to know that her carefree attitude was a cover for pain over years of estrangement from her father. She and her husband, also a seminarian, were musically gifted. They had brought up two sons and a daughter.

Mona had considered joining Connie and her teenage daughter to visit another seminary friend, Allegra, now a missionary in Mexico City. Mona had visited there before, as well as Allegra's earlier missionary postings in Africa, Nicaragua and the Dominican Republic. The trip with Connie had fallen through, which Mona realized was probably good since her summer had been remarkably hectic. Also, she knew that Allegra made periodic trips to the US and never failed to visit.

For many months at seminary, Allegra had been just a face Mona recognized from passing hellos in the hall. Then one night someone knocked at the Cartwright front door. It was another student, Annette. "Please come and help Allegra," she implored. "She is sick with a high fever and can't stop coughing." Mona had gathered up Epsom salts, turpentine, Vicks salve, Vaseline and onions and hastened with Annette to Allegra's dorm. Mona drew a tub of tepid water, added Epsom salts and had Allegra placed in the tub. She soaked a towel with the salve, turpentine and Vaseline and covered Allegra's chest. The fresh onions were placed strategically around the bedroom. Noticeable improvement began quickly. That night began a close and enduring relationship. Haitian-born Allegra told Mona, "And I was told by my people that black Americans were no friends of ours!" Allegra would more than repay Mona as time passed, on one occasion nursing her through a case of the flu and later spending an entire summer caring for her during a post-surgical recovery.

Annette was the third seminary student with whom Mona had remained close. The daughter of an Army sergeant, she was knowledgeable and well-travelled. In class she was quick to offer contrary opinions, and it didn't matter whether she was disagreeing with faculty or fellow students. Or even her mother, who had expressed disappointment at Annette's vocational choice. "I refuse to kowtow to anyone simply to be highly favored," she asserted. Consequently she was not well favored by most of the seminary community. However one student, a young Haitian, favored her plenty, and the two married. They had two sons of their own and adopted a daughter.

A recent note from Annette had been a jolting reminder of fleeting time. "Mama Mona, thank you for the beautiful dress." Mona had sent a lovely white dress to Annette in Haiti on the occasion of her upcoming wedding anniversary. "You were there for us in the beginning and now you are here to cheer us on after 30 years," Annette's note continued. "We are so blessed by your love."

Three decades! Mona was taken aback at the span of time since seminary days when her special friendships with Annette, Allegra and Connie had started. All three young women had blossomed into ardent servants of the Lord! Mona thought of the saying that change is the only life experience that remains constant. True, she thought, and oh how the Lord works through change. Going to seminary had involved enormous change for Mona. Could it possibly be that God put her in that place to help prepare some of His disciples for service?

There were others with whom she had lost touch. Students she had taught in school and Bible studies. Wild George, who had come in anger, sat on her front porch as she calmly witnessed, and gone away hungering for righteousness. How wonderful and mysterious are God's ways of working.

\*\*\*

A few weeks later Mona was again enjoying her porch retreat, having just returned from a reunion cruise of the extended Cartwright family. Children, grandchildren, great grandchildren and more distant relations had been there in abundance. She exulted in their nearness and the obvious fun they were sharing. As she watched her progeny celebrate family, she mentally paraphrased the promise of Psalm 127 – *Children are a heritage of the Lord and happy is the woman who has a quiver full of them.* Praise God, she thought. *I have been blessed beyond measure.*

Yet for Mona, the joy of the cruise was quietness and solitude rather than festivities. More than anything else, she cherished hours on the deck outside her cabin, reading, meditating and nodding off now and then. The younger generations scampered all over the ship, taking in every activity and diversion. That's why people came on cruises now, she thought to herself. It was all so loud, frantic and busy. Whatever happened to the refined, relaxed leisure that once made cruising so delightful?

Part of the change, she knew, was her own age. Now in her 90s, she found it a challenge to get around the enormous ship. When passengers went ashore to enjoy a Caribbean beach, for Mona the white sand and blue waters were lovely to see but difficult to move through.

Thankfully, age's influence on her vitality was purely physical. Mona still loved her book club, both the social time with friends and the opportunity to tackle difficult subjects. Her twice-weekly Bridge sessions continued to be a joy, win or lose. Church responsibilities, including her very active Bible study group and her prayer circle, she embraced with vigor and purpose.

"Yes," she exclaimed. "Life has reached its fullness." Decades earlier, ill and hospitalized, Mona had started discovering what it meant to live in the Big Picture that Fr. Rohr described. "Connected to the whole." "Broader and deeper." The process of discovery had continued and expanded, through events and experiences that were by turns beautiful, ugly, amazing, strange, joyful, disappointing, overwhelming and mundane. By God's incomprehensible work of Grace, He had transformed her life into one of outward focus, committed to service to His people.

In her late years, the quiet porch refreshed her like nothing else. It inspired her to ponder her life's meaning – past, present and future. The past was to be learned from. The present and future were still hers to influence.

"Nothing but character" – that long-ago description of the Randalls came back to her thoughts, along with vivid memories of her parents' dire circumstances. The Cartwrights had character, and plenty more, thank God. Not only had her children and grandchildren attained material comfort that Madeline and Josiah could never have imagined – they were footprints in the world. They could be found among the heroes and sheroes of law, medicine, education, civic and community activism. Each Cartwright generation had produced ministers. Looking ahead, she smiled to think that 13 great grandchildren were coming along to take their own places as leaders and contributors. The Randalls' descendants were marching to the beat of the drum.

Mona's thoughts often returned to the life she had shared with Doug, and she did not shrink from recounting the bitter as well as the sweet. Bitterness was a truer teacher, she believed. As with most every experience since her theophany, her memories were framed by scriptural truth.

The darkness of Doug's moods – "jealousy is cruel as the grave; the coals thereof are coals of fire, which hath a most vehement flame." Song of Solomon 8:6

The guilty escape she briefly found with Anthony – "stolen waters are sweet, and bread eaten in secret is pleasant." Proverbs 9:17

The inevitable power of truth – "there is nothing covered or hidden that will not be known." Mark 4:22

Even now, she shook her head in confoundment at the

profound change in Doug once she had confessed the affair. At first, pleasure in vindication, "I knew it! I knew I wasn't crazy!" Mona had gone on to emphasize that his relentless accusations over ten years had been dead wrong, and the affair was a single desperate reaction. It was as if a fog lifted, leaving him free of the pain and anxiety that had been his master since boyhood. Now, Mona praised God for truth that had lifted both of their burdens – his of suspicion and distrust, hers of guilt. Fr. Rohr wrote honest words, "Before the truth sets you free, it tends to make you miserable." The misery had dissolved in freedom, and then into love beyond passion.

Her thoughts once again ran to a passage which had become her favorite.

"So we do not lose heart. Though our outer nature is wasting away, our inner nature is being renewed every day. For this slight momentary affliction is preparing us for an eternal weight of glory beyond all comparison, because we look not to the things that are seen but to the things that are unseen; for the things that are seen are fleeting, but the things that are unseen are eternal. For we know that if the earthly tent we live in is destroyed, we have a building from God, a house not made with hands, eternal in the heavens. Here indeed we groan, and long to put on our heavenly dwelling so that by putting it on we may not be found naked.  For while we are still in this tent, we sigh with anxiety, not that we would be unclothed, but that we would be further clothed, so that what is mortal may be swallowed up by life.  He who has prepared us for this very thing is God, who has given us the Spirit as a guarantee."

2nd Corinthians 4:16-5:5

How amazing, she thought, to be beyond losing heart, beyond fearing the wasting of age.  Whatever days remained for her, each would be another day of becoming prepared, another day in the company of the Spirit.

*Eva R. Bird*

## ABOUT THE AUTHOR

Eva R. Bird is affectionately known as "Mother Bird" and unofficially dubbed as "Rev. Eva" because of her extensive Biblical knowledge, and her gifts of teaching, exhortation, and spiritual counseling.  She has served faithfully as a pillar and "Mother" of the church at St. Paul's Episcopal Church in Atlanta, GA, where she has resided for the past twenty five years. This is her first novel.

Eva Ruth Brown Bird was married to and served as a partner in ministry and in life with the late Rev. Dr. VanS. Bird for 66 years.  Together they organized several churches, and she has continued to the present day to lead Bible Study, spiritual growth groups, and retreats for persons of all ages and backgrounds, particularly women. Active in community affairs, she has volunteered at local local elementary schools and continues to co-facilitate spiritual growth groups at state women's prisons. Eva has three children, eleven grandchildren, and seventeen great-grandchildren.

Eva began her professional career teaching junior high school in 1961, and ended her career teaching first grade, remaining at the same school in the same classroom for 16 years until she retired in 1985. She received a BA in Sociology from Fort Valley College, a Masters in Early Childhood Education from Temple University, and a Masters Degree in Religion from Eastern Baptist at Theological Seminary (now Palmer Theological Seminary).

Eva is widely traveled and has visited several countries in all continents except Australia and Antarctica. Her greatest joy and passion has been in counseling and mentoring young women throughout the years of her ministry. Her guiding scripture for this calling is:
"Guide older women into lives of reverence so that they may end up as ... models of goodness. By looking at them the younger women will know how to love their husbands and children, be virtuous, and pure." Titus 2:3 – 4, MSG.

MONA

www.ingramcontent.com/pod-product-compliance
Lightning Source LLC
Chambersburg PA
CBHW020326200626
46814CB00006BB/2435